The Fall

Albert Camus was born in Algeria in 1913. He studied philosophy at the University of Algiers, then became a journalist, as well as organizing the *Theatre de l'équipe*, a young avant-garde dramatic group. His early essays were collected in *L'Envers et l'endroit* (*The Wrong Side and the Right Side*) and *Noces* (*Nuptials*). As a young man, he went to Paris, where he worked on the newspaper *Paris Soir* before returning to Algiers. His play, *Caligula*, appeared in 1939, while his first two important books, *L'Etranger* (*The Outsider*) and the philosophical essays collected in *Le Mythe de Sisyphe* (*The Myth of Sisyphus*), were published when he returned to Paris. After the occupation of France by the Germans in 1940, Camus became one of the intellectual leaders of the Resistance movement. He edited and contributed to the underground newspaper *Combat*, which he had helped to found. After the war, he devoted himself to writing and established an international reputation with such books as *La Peste* (*The Plague*) (1947), *Les Justes* (*The Just*) (1949) and *La Chute* (*The Fall*) (1956). During the late 1950s, Camus renewed his active interest in the theatre, writing and directing stage adaptations of William Faulkner's *Requiem for a Nun* and Dostoyevsky's *The Possessed*. He was awarded the Nobel Prize for Literature in 1957. Camus was killed in a road accident in 1960. His last novel, *Le Premier Homme* (*The First Man*), unfinished at the time of his death, appeared for the first time in 1994. An instant bestseller, the book received widespread critical acclaim, and has been translated and published in over thirty countries. Much of Camus' work is available in Penguin.

Robin Buss has translated several works for Penguin, including a selection of writings by Sartre and Camus' *The Plague*. His translation of Henri Barbusse's *Under Fire* was shortlisted for the Weidenfeld Translation Prize. He has also written books on the French and Italian cinema.

ALBERT CAMUS

The Fall

Translated by ROBIN BUSS

PENGUIN BOOKS

PENGUIN CLASSICS

UK | USA | Canada | Ireland | Australia
India | New Zealand | South Africa

Penguin Books is part of the Penguin Random House group of companies
whose addresses can be found at global.penguinrandomhouse.com.

First published in France as *La Chute* 1956
This translation first published in Great Britain in Penguin Classics 2006
This edition published in Penguin Classics 2013
017

Printed in Great Britain by Clays Ltd, St Ives plc

ISBN: 978-0-141-18794-5

www.greenpenguin.co.uk

MIX
Paper from
responsible sources
FSC
www.fsc.org   FSC™ C018179

Penguin Books is committed to a sustainable
future for our business, our readers and our planet.
This book is made from Forest Stewardship
Council™ certified paper.

The Fall

My good sir, I wonder if I might venture to offer you some help? Otherwise, I'm afraid you may not be able to make yourself understood by the worthy gorilla who presides over the comings and goings of this establishment: he only speaks Dutch. Unless you allow me to plead your case, he won't guess that you want some gin. There: I dare to hope that he has got the message. That nod of the head should mean that my argument has won his ear. He's off, look: making haste slowly, the clever chap. You're lucky: he didn't complain. When he refuses to serve you, he just grunts. No one argues with that. It's the privilege of these big beasts to be moody when they like. I'm off, Monsieur, and glad to have been of service. Thank you; I'd accept if I were sure that I should not be imposing on you. You're too kind. I'll put my glass here, then, at your table.

You're right: his silence is deafening. It's the silence of the primeval forest, heavy with menace. It surprises me at times, the obstinacy with which our uncommunicative friend insists on giving the cold shoulder to every civilized language. His work involves serving sailors of all nationalities in this bar – which, for some reason or other, though we're in Amsterdam, he calls Mexico City. With a job like that, wouldn't you think his ignorance might be a burden to him? Imagine Cro-Magnon Man taking rooms in the Tower of Babel. He'd feel a little out of his element, to say the least. But no, this fellow doesn't feel like an exile, he just carries on regardless. One of the few remarks that I have heard him utter was to declare that you could take it or leave it. Take or leave what? Our friend himself, quite likely. I must confess, I've got a soft spot for these people who are all of a piece. When you have thought deeply about mankind, whether because it's your job or your vocation to do so, you may sometimes feel a certain nostalgia for these primates. There's no side to them.

Actually, that's not quite true of our friend here, though any grudges that he harbours run pretty deep. Not understanding what is said in his presence has given him a suspicious nature. Hence that air of nervous gravity, as though he did at least suspect that not everything was quite right with people. This outlook makes it harder to talk to him about whatever is unconnected with his job. Take that empty rectangle on the back wall above his head which shows where a picture used to hang. There was a picture there once, a particularly interesting one, a real masterpiece. Well, I happened to be here when the master of the house took it in and when he let it go. In both cases, it was with the same mistrust, after weeks of rumination. One has to admit that on that score society has somewhat tarnished the pure simplicity of his character.

Mind you, I'm not passing judgement. I view his mistrust as well founded and would happily share it, were it not, as you can see, contrary to my own sociable nature to do so. Alas, I'm a chatterbox and I make friends easily. Although I do know how to keep a respectful distance, I seize any opportunity. When I was living in France, were I to meet an intelligent man, I could not but get to know him. Ah, I saw you flinch at that turn of phrase: I must admit to a weakness for the subjunctive mode and for fine language in general. I'm not proud of it, believe me. I know quite well that a liking for clean linen does not necessarily imply that one has dirty feet. No matter. Style, like poplin, all too often conceals eczema. I console myself with the thought that, after all, those who stammer are not blameless, either. Yes, yes, let's have some more gin.

Will you be staying long in Amsterdam? Lovely town, don't you think? Fascinating? There's an adjective I haven't heard for a long time. Since I left Paris, in fact, and that was years ago. But the heart remembers, and I have forgotten nothing of our beautiful capital or its *quais*. Paris is an authentic *trompe-l'œil*, a splendid stage set inhabited by four million extras. Nearly five million, at the last census? Well, well, they must have been breeding. It wouldn't surprise me. I always thought our fellow citizens were crazy about two things: ideas and fornication. This way and that, as it were. In any case, we shouldn't judge them badly for it. They're not the only ones – it's like that all over Europe. I sometimes try to imagine what future historians will say about us. They'll be able to sum up modern man in a single sentence: he fornicated and read the papers. After that robust description, I should guess there will be no more to say on the subject.

The Dutch? Oh, no, they're a lot less modern. Look at them: they can take their time. What are they doing? Well, those gentlemen live by the labour of these women. Actually, male and female, they are the most respectable of creatures, who have come here as they always do, because of some mythomanic illusion or through sheer stupidity: in short, through too much imagination or too little. From time to time, the gentlemen indulge in a little sport with the knife or the revolver, but don't imagine that they care for it. The role demands it, that's all, and they are dying with fright as they shoot off their last rounds. Having said which, I do find them more moral than the others,

5

the ones who keep their killing in the family and do it by dribs and drabs. Don't you think that our society is designed to kill in that way? Of course, you've surely heard about those tiny fish in the rivers of Brazil which attack the rash swimmer by the thousands, eat him up in a few moments in quick little mouthfuls and leave only a perfectly clean skeleton behind? So, that's the way they're constituted. 'Do you want a clean life, like everyone else?' Of course, you answer yes. How could you not? 'Fine. We'll clean you up. Here's a job, here's a family, here's some organized leisure.' And the little teeth bite into the flesh, right down to the bone. But I'm being unfair. I shouldn't have said, 'the way they're constituted', because after all, it's our way, too: it's a case of who strips whom.

At least, our gin is coming. To your health! Yes, the gorilla said something: he called me Doctor. In this country, everyone's a doctor or professor. They like to show respect, out of kindness or modesty. At least, malice is not a national institution here. As it happens, I'm not a doctor. If you want to know, I was a lawyer before I came here. Now I'm a judge-penitent.

But let me introduce myself: Jean-Baptiste Clamence, at your service. Delighted to meet you. You must be in business? More or less? Excellent reply. Judicious, too: we're only *more or less* in anything. Now, let me play detective. You are roughly my age, with that resigned look of the forty-year-old who has pretty well seen it all; you're more or less well dressed, as people are in our country, and you have soft hands. So; more or less middle class! But refined middle class. To flinch at a subjunctive shows twice over how cultured you are, firstly because you recognize it and then because it irritates you. Finally, you find me entertaining, which, if I may say, implies open-mindedness on your part. So you are more or less . . . But what matter? Professions interest me less than sects. Let me ask you two questions – but only answer if you don't think I'm being inquisitive. Are you wealthy? Fairly? Good. And do you share your wealth with the poor? No. Well, that means you are what I call a Sadducee. If you don't know your Bible, I realize that that will not mean much to you. Ah, it does? So you do know your Bible? You really do interest me.

As for me . . . Well, you can judge for yourself. With my build, my shoulders and this face, which I've often been told is a bit fierce, I suppose I look rather like a rugby player, don't I? But if you judge me by my conversation, you must admit I'm quite cultured. The camel that supplied the hide for my coat must have been a mangy beast, while I, on the other hand, am well manicured. What's more, I know what's what and yet here I am confiding in you, unguardedly, just because of your face. And, despite my good manners and fine speech, I hang around the sailors' bars in Zeedijk. There, give up. Mine is a double job, that's all, just as humans are double. As I told you, I'm a judge-penitent. One thing only is simple in my case, which is that I own nothing. Yes, I was rich, and no, I didn't share anything with other people. What does that prove? That I, too, was a Sadducee . . . Ah! Can you hear the sirens in the port? There'll be fog tonight on the Zuyder Zee.

Are you leaving already? Forgive me if I kept you. If you'll allow me, I'd like to pay. You're my guest in Mexico City and I've been very happy to welcome you here. I'll certainly be here tomorrow, as I am every evening, and I'll gratefully accept your invitation. Which way? Well . . . Would you object – it would be the simplest thing – if I were to accompany you as far as the port? From there, if you go round the Jewish quarter, you'll come to those fine avenues where they have trams loaded with flowers and music blaring out of them. Your hotel is on one of them, the Damrak. After you, please. I live in the Jewish quarter, or what they called the Jewish quarter until our Hitlerite brethren cleared a space in it. What a clean-up! Seventy-five thousand Jews deported or murdered: that's vacuum cleaning. I admire such diligence, such methodical patience! You have to be methodical when you have no character. Here, the method worked wonders, there's no denying it: I live on the site of one of the greatest crimes in history. Perhaps that's what helps me to understand our gorilla and why he's so mistrustful. I have the same ability to resist the natural bent that inevitably inclines me to like people. When I see a new face, something sets off an alarm bell inside me. 'Slow down! Danger!' Even when the attraction is strongest, I am on my guard.

Do you know that in my little village, in the course of some reprisals, a German officer politely asked an old woman to choose which of her two sons was to be shot as a hostage? Can you imagine choosing like that? This one? No, the other one. And seeing him leave. I don't want to dwell on it, but believe me, sir, anything can happen, however surprising. I knew one pure heart that refused mistrust. He was a pacifist, a libertarian, who loved all mankind and all animals equally. Yes, an exceptional soul, there's no doubt of it. Well, during the last religious wars in Europe he retired to the country. There he wrote over the door of his house: 'Wherever you come from welcome and enter.' And who do you suppose answered his invitation? Why, militiamen, who marched in, made themselves at home and disembowelled him.

Oh, excuse me, Madame! Mind you, she didn't understand a thing. So many people, eh? At this time of night, and despite the rain which has been falling for days. Thankfully, there's gin, the only light in this darkness. Do you feel the golden, copper light it puts inside you? I like to walk through the town, after dark, wrapped in the warmth of gin. I walk for nights on end, dreaming or talking interminably to myself. Like this evening – yes, and

I'm afraid I'm rather overwhelming you . . . Thank you, you're most kind. But it's an overflow: as soon as I open my mouth, the words pour out. What's more, this country inspires me. I like its people, swarming around on the pavements, wedged into their little space of houses and water, encircled by mists, cold earth and a sea that steams like damp washing. I like them because they are double. They are both here and somewhere else.

Of course! Listening to their heavy steps on the moist paving, seeing them go ponderously by between their shops which are full of golden herrings and jewels the colour of dead leaves, I suppose you think they're here, this evening? You're like every-one else, you probably imagine that these good people are a tribe of town councillors and merchants, counting up their guilders with their chances of eternal life, whose only poetic interlude consists in taking anatomy lessons while wearing broad-brimmed hats. You're wrong. They are walking beside us, agreed, yet look where their heads are: in that fog of neon, gin and mint pouring off the red and green shop signs. Holland is a reverie, sir, a dream of gold and smoke, more smoky by day and golden at night, while night and day this reverie is filled with Lohengrins like these, dreamily going past on their black bicycles with high handlebars, funerary swans endlessly drifting past, throughout the country, around the sea, along the canals. They are dream-ing, their heads in their copper clouds, they ride around, they pray, like sleepwalkers in the gilded incense of the mist, and they are no longer here. They have departed, to travel thousands of kilometres away, to Java, the distant isle. They pray to those grimacing gods of Indonesia which they have set up in all their windows and which, at this moment, are drifting around above our heads before alighting, like resplendent monkeys, on the shop signs and stepped roofs, to remind these nostalgic colonials that Holland is not only the Europe of the counting-house, but the sea, the sea that leads to Cipango and those islands where men die happy and insane.

But I'm getting carried away, I'm making my case! Forgive me. Habit, sir, the profession – and also my desire to help you really understand this town and the heart of the matter! Because we are at the heart of the matter. Have you noticed that the concentric canals of Amsterdam are like the circles of hell? A bourgeois hell, inhabited of course by bad dreams. When you come here from outside, as you go through these circles, life – and its crimes with it – becomes denser and more obscure. Here we are in the last circle, the circle of . . . Ha! You know that? Damn! You're getting harder to pin down. But then you understand why I can say that the centre of things is here, even though we are at the far end of the continent. A sensitive man understands such peculiarities. In any case, the readers of newspapers and the fornicators cannot go further. They come from the four corners of Europe and halt around the inner sea, on the bleached shore. They listen to the sirens and look in vain for the shapes of boats in the fog, then they go back through the rain. Chilled to the marrow, they come and ask for gin at Mexico City, in every language. There, I wait for them.

Until tomorrow, then, my good sir and dear compatriot. No, you can find your own way from here on, I'll leave you at the bridge. I never cross a bridge at night – because of a vow. After all, what would happen if someone were to jump in the water? One of two things could happen: you would go in after, to fish the person out, and in cold weather it could be the death of you. Or you would abandon the poor creature; but repressing an urge to dive can lead to strange sorts of cramp. Good night! What? Those ladies behind the windows? Dreams, sir, inexpensive dreams, a voyage to the Indies! They perfume themselves with spices. You go inside, they close the curtains and the ship sets sail. The gods come down on the naked bodies and the islands are cast deliriously adrift, crowned with a tousled mop of palm trees tossed by the wind. Try it, do.

What is a judge-penitent? Ah, I got you interested with that. Believe me, I meant no harm by it. I can explain the business more clearly. In a sense, that is one of my jobs. But first of all I must describe a certain number of things which will help you better to understand what I have to say.

A few years ago, I was a lawyer in Paris – and, I must say, rather a well-known one. Of course, I didn't tell you my real name. I specialized, in good causes. Widows and orphans, as they say; though I'm not sure why, because there are abusive widows and vicious orphans. However, all I needed was to sniff the odour of victimization on a defendant to swing into action. And what action! A storm! I wore my heart on my sleeve. You would have really thought that justice slept with me every night. I'm sure you would have admired the precisely judged tone, the precisely judged emotion, the fervour and power of persuasion, and the controlled indignation of my speeches for the defence. Nature has favoured me in appearance, and it requires no effort for me to strike a noble pose. Apart from which, I was sustained by two sincere feelings: the satisfaction of being on the right side in court and an instinctive contempt for judges as a class. Well, perhaps the contempt was not so instinctive after all. I realize now that there were reasons for it. But to the outside observer, it seemed like something of a passion. There's no denying that, at least for the moment, judges are necessary, don't you agree? And yet I couldn't understand how a man could appoint himself to exercise that surprising office. I had to accept it, since I saw it, but rather in the way that I accepted locusts . . . with the difference that the invasions of those orthoptera have never brought me a penny, while I used to earn my living by conversing with people whom I despised.

However. I was on the right side, and that was enough to ease my conscience. A sense of legality, the satisfaction of being right and the joy of self-esteem: these, my dear sir, are powerful incentives to keep us on our feet and moving forward. On the other hand, if you deprive men of these, you transform them into rabid dogs. How many crimes have been committed for no other reason than that the perpetrator could not bear being in the wrong! I once knew an industrialist who had a perfect wife, the object of universal admiration, and yet he was unfaithful to her. The man literally raged at being in the wrong, of not being awarded or being able to award himself a certificate of good conduct. The more perfect his wife appeared, the more furious he became. In the end, his wrongness became unbearable to him. So what do you think he did? He gave up being unfaithful? No. He killed her. That's how I came to meet him.

My situation was more enviable. Not only did I not run any risk of joining the ranks of criminals (in particular, I had no chance of killing my wife, since I was a bachelor), but I would also only take their cases on the sole condition that they were good murderers, as others are noble savages. I got great satisfaction from the very way I conducted the defence. I was really beyond reproach in my professional life. Needless to say, I never took bribes, but neither did I stoop to any other kind of dealings. What is rarer still, I never agreed to flatter any journalist so that he would write favourably about me, or any civil servant whose friendship might be advantageous. I was even fortunate enough to be offered the Legion of Honour two or three times, refusing it with a discreet dignity which was my true reward. Finally, I never made a poor client pay, nor did I advertise that fact. Please don't think, my dear sir, that I'm boasting about all this. It was no credit to me: I have always mocked the greed which, in our society, takes the place of ambition. I was aiming higher: you will see that the phrase is accurate in my case.

Already, you may see how self-satisfied I was. I enjoyed my own being, and we all know that this means happiness – even though, so as not to irritate one another, we sometimes pretend to condemn such pleasure and describe it as egotism. I did at least enjoy the part of my being that responded so precisely to the widow and the orphan that in the end, through constant exercise, it came to govern all my life. For example, I loved to help blind men across the street. Seeing from afar a white stick trembling on the edge of the pavement, I would dash foward, sometimes getting in a second before some charitable hand that was already reaching out, whisk the blind person away from any sympathetic attentions other than my own and lead him with a soft, but firm, grasp over the crossing, weaving among the traffic, towards the safe haven of the opposite pavement, where we would part with mutual feelings of gratitude. Similarly, I have always liked to direct people in the street, give them a light, offer a helping hand with a heavy barrow, push a broken-down car and buy a newspaper from a Salvation Army man or flowers from an old woman, even though I knew she had stolen them from the Montparnasse cemetery. I also liked – though I find this even harder to admit – I liked to give to beggars. A friend of mine, a great Christian, agreed that your first reaction when you see a beggar coming towards your door is unpleasant. Well, with me it was worse: I rejoiced. Let's say no more.

I'd rather speak of my good manners. They were famous,

beyond dispute. And indeed, being polite was a great joy to me. If the opportunity arose some mornings for me to give up my seat on the bus or the métro to someone who obviously deserved it, or to pick up something that an old lady had dropped and to return it to her with a smile that I knew only too well, or merely to give up my taxi to a person who was in more of a hurry than I was, then my whole day would be lit up by it. I have to confess that I even welcomed those days when there was a public transport strike, providing me with the opportunity to stop my car and pick up some of my unfortunate fellow citizens, stranded at the bus stops on their way home. In short, giving up my seat in the theatre so that a couple could be reunited or, on a journey, lifting a young woman's bag into the rack that was too high for her were deeds that I performed more often than other people, because I more often kept an eye open for the opportunity to do so and gained greater pleasure from it.

I was also, rightly, thought to be generous. I gave a good deal, both publicly and privately. But far from suffering when I had to relinquish an object or a sum of money, I derived constant pleasure from it, not the least part of which was a kind of melancholy that sometimes rose up within me when I thought of the sterility of these gifts and the probable ingratitude that they occasioned. I even felt such pleasure in giving that I hated to be obliged to do so. I was bored by a precise attention to matters of money and engaged in them with irritation. I needed to be the master of my generosity.

These are small touches, but they will help you to realize the continual delights that I experienced in life and above all in my work. To be stopped in the corridors of the law courts, for example, by the wife of a defendant whom one has represented simply out of justice or pity, by which I mean for free, and hearing this woman murmur that nothing, no, nothing can repay

15

what one has done for them, and then replying that it was quite normal, anyone would have done as much and even offering assistance in getting through the hard days ahead, and after that, to cut short her outpourings of gratitude, so as to ensure that they don't lose their proper resonance, kissing the poor woman's hand and leaving – that, believe me, my dear sir, is to reach a point above mere ambition and to rise to the highest summit, where virtue is no longer sustained by anything but itself.

Let us pause on these lofty peaks. You understand now what I meant when I spoke about aiming higher. I was referring to these high summits, the only place where I can live. Yes, I have never felt so much at home as up there, at the top. Even in the minutiae of daily life, I needed to be up above. I preferred the bus to the métro, hansom cabs to taxis and balconies to mezzanines. As someone who loved light aircraft with open cockpits, I was also the person whom you would always see on boats pacing the poop deck. In the highlands, I avoided enclosed valleys and headed for the passes or the plateaux; I was the man of the high ridges, at the very least. If fate had forced me to choose a manual job, take my word for it, I'd have been a tiler rather than a turner and embraced vertigo to work on the rooftops. I had a horror of bunkers, holds, tunnels, caves and chasms. I even felt a special loathing for speleologists who had the cheek to appear on the front pages of newspapers and whose exploits disgusted me. Trying to reach a depth of eight hundred metres at the risk of getting one's head stuck in a gully of rock – or 'siphon', as those crazies call it – seemed to me the act of a person who was either perverted or deranged. There was something criminal about it.

By contrast, a natural balcony, five or six hundred metres above a sea that was still visible and bathed in sunlight, was the place where I felt most at ease, especially if I was alone, high above the human ants. I had no difficulty in appreciating why sermons, thunderous homilies and miracles of fire took place on inaccessible heights. In my view, one could not meditate in cellars or prison cells (unless the latter were situated in towers, with an extensive view). One could only rot. I could understand the man who, after taking holy orders, renounced his vows because his cell, instead of opening as he had expected on a wide landscape, faced a blank wall. You may be sure that, in my case, I did not rot. At every moment of the day, whether I was alone or with other people, I climbed the heights, I lit bonfires up there and heard the joyous acclaim rising up towards me. So at least I relished life and my own superiority.

Fortunately, my profession satisfied this call to the heights. It relieved me of any bitterness towards my fellow man, whom I constantly put under an obligation without ever owing him anything. It set me above the judge, whom I judged in his turn, and above the accused, whom I compelled to feel gratitude. Mark this well, sir: I lived with impunity. No judgement affected me: I was not an actor on the stage of the courtroom, but somewhere in the flies like those gods who are lowered from time to time by mechanical means, so that they can raise the performance to a new level and give it sense. After all, living above the rest is still the only way to be seen and saluted by the greatest number.

As a matter of fact, some of my fine criminals had responded to the same feeling when they killed. In their sad predicament, reading the newspapers doubtless brought them a kind of miserable consolation. Like many men, they could no longer bear anonymity and their impatience may have been partly responsible for driving them to regrettable extremes. In fact, if you want to get yourself known, all you have to do is to kill your concierge. Unfortunately, the reputation you gain will prove ephemeral, because there are so many concierges who deserve the knife – and get it. Crime is constantly in the spotlight, but one criminal only makes a fleeting appearance before immediately being replaced. In short, these brief triumphs are too costly. Defending these unfortunate seekers after reputation, on the contrary, meant being truly recognized, at the same time and in the same places, but with greater economy of means. This also encouraged me to exert worthy efforts to ensure that they would pay as little as possible: the cost to them, whatever it was, they paid in a certain manner in my place. Conversely, the indignation, talent and emotion that I expended relieved me of any debt towards them. Judges punished the crime, the accused atoned for it, and I, free of all responsibility, beyond judgement or punishment, reigned at liberty, bathed in a prelapsarian glow.

Isn't that what Eden was, my dear sir: a direct line to life? Mine was like that. I never needed to learn how to live. I knew everything about it as soon as I was born. There are people whose problem is to protect themselves from other men or at least to come to terms with them. In my case, the terms were fixed. Familiar when I needed to be, silent when that was necessary and capable of being both easy-going and serious, I was always in tune with my surroundings. As a result, I was very popular and enjoyed great social success. I was not bad-looking and could be both a tireless dancer and an unobtrusive scholar, as well as managing simultaneously to love women and justice, which is no easy matter; and I practised sport and the fine arts . . . in short, I'll say no more in case you might suspect me of being smug. But I ask you to imagine a man in the prime of life, in perfect health, many-talented, skilled in physical exercise as well as in the exercise of the mind, neither poor nor rich, who sleeps soundly and is deeply satisfied with himself, yet shows it only in pleasant sociability. So I think you must allow me to speak, in all modesty, of a successful life.

Yes, few creatures have been more natural than I was. I was

in total harmony with life; I cohered with it in its entirety from top to bottom, denying none of its ironies, its greatness or its servitude. In particular, physical matter, the flesh which troubles or depresses so many men in love or solitude, brought me unremitting delight without enslaving me. I was made to have a body. Hence that harmony, that relaxed mastery that people felt in me and which, they would sometimes admit, helped them to live. They sought my company. For example, strangers would often think they had met me before. Life, its creatures and its gifts came to me and I accepted these tokens of esteem with benevolent pride. In fact, through being a man in such fullness and simplicity, I felt I was something of a superman.

I came from a respectable, though humble, family (my father was an army officer), yet there were mornings, I have to confess in all modesty, when I felt I was the son of a king, or a burning bush. Mind you, this was something different from the conviction I enjoyed of being more intelligent than anyone else. Besides, this conviction was pointless, since so many idiots also possess it. No, the more I was blessed, the more I felt – though I hesitate to admit this – chosen, personally chosen, above all others, for this long, enduring success. In reality, this was a result of my modesty. I refused to attribute my success to sole personal merit and I could not believe that the combination of such different and such extreme qualities in a single being was the result of pure chance. This is why I lived happily and felt, in some way, entitled to this happiness by a command from on high. When I tell you that I was not at all a religious person, you will appreciate even better how extraordinary that certainty was. Ordinary or not, it lifted me for a long time above the daily round, and for years I literally soared – years for which, to tell the truth, I still pine. I soared, until the evening when . . . But, no, that's another matter; we must forget it. Besides, I could be exaggerating. It's true: I was at ease in everything, yet satisfied with nothing. Each joy made me yearn for another. I went from one party to the next. There were times when I danced for nights on end, more and more intoxicated with people and life. Sometimes, late in those nights of dancing, slightly tipsy, my frenzy and the mad abandonment of those around me drove me into a rapture that was at once weary and satiated, so that it appeared to me, in the extreme of fatigue, that I finally understood the secret of life and the world. But by the following morning the weariness had vanished and with it the secret; so I was off again . . . In that way, I kept on running, always nourished, never full, not knowing when to stop, until the day, or rather the evening when the music stopped and the lights went out. The party at which I had once been happy . . . But let me call on our friend, the apeman. Nod your head to thank him and, above all, drink with me because I need your sympathy.

I can see that you're surprised at my saying that. Have you never had a sudden need for sympathy, for help or for friendship? Of course you have. I have learned to make do with sympathy. It is easier to come by and it carries no commitment. In the internal monologue, 'please accept my sympathy' comes right before 'now let's get on with something else'. It's the emotion felt by a prime minister or company chairman: you get it cheap after some disaster. Friendship is not so easy: it's long and hard to win, but when it's there, you can't get rid of it, you have to make do. In any case, don't imagine that your friends will be phoning you up every evening, as they should, to find out if this happens to be the day you've decided to commit suicide or simply need company or don't feel like going out. No, no, don't worry. If they do phone, it will be the day when you're not alone and life is smiling on you. As for suicide, they're more likely to drive you to it, by reason of what, according to them, you owe yourself. Heaven preserve us, my dear sir, from being put on a pedestal by our friends. As for those whose role it is to love us – I mean, relatives and in-laws (what a word!) – it's a different tune. They find the right word, but it's usually the one that wounds. They pick up the phone to you like someone picking up a gun. And their aim is on target. Oh, those Bazaines!

What? Which evening? I'll get to it, give me time. Actually, in a way, I'm on the subject with this business of friends and relations. You see, I was told about a man whose friend was put in jail and who slept on the floor of his bedroom every night so that he would not be enjoying a luxury that had been denied to the friend whom he loved. Who would sleep on the floor for us, my dear sir? Am I myself capable of it? Let me tell you, I'd like to be and I shall be. Yes, we'll all be capable of it one day and that will be our salvation. But it's not easy, because friendship is absent-minded or at least powerless. It cannot achieve what it wants. Perhaps, after all, it doesn't want strongly enough. Perhaps we do not love life enough. Have you observed that only death awakens our feelings? How we love the friends who have just departed – don't you find? How we admire those of our masters who have been silenced, their mouths full of dirt! Then our tributes come naturally, tributes that they may have waited all their lives to hear. But do you know why we are always fairer and more generous towards the dead? The reason is simple! We have no obligation where they're concerned! They leave us free, we can take our time, fit the tribute into the interval between cocktails and a nice mistress, in other words, lost moments. If they did oblige us to do anything, it would be to remember, and our memories are short. No, what we like in our friends is fresh death, painful death, our own feelings, in short, ourselves!

So I used to have a friend whom I avoided most of the time. He got on my nerves a little and he had a conscience. But on his deathbed, we were reunited, don't you worry! I didn't miss a day. He died, happy with me, holding my hand. A woman who used to chase after me too much, in vain, had the good taste to die young. How much room there was for her in my heart! And when, in addition to that, it's a suicide! Good lord, what a commotion! The phone rings, your heart is overflowing, and there are those phrases, deliberately brief, but loaded with meaning, and the controlled grief and, yes, even a little self-accusation!

That's what men are like, sir: two-faced: they cannot love unless they love themselves. Watch your neighbours when there happens to be a death in the building. They were sleeping through their little lives and then, for example, the concierge dies. All at once, they're wide awake, quivering, asking for news, feeling sorry. A death is announced and at last the curtain goes up. They need tragedy; after all, it's their little moment of transcendence, their aperitif. Actually, it may be no accident if I mention a concierge. I had one, a real brute, the essence of bile, the epitome of insignificance and bitterness who would have tried the patience of a saint. I was no longer on speaking terms with him, but his very existence threatened my accustomed enjoyment of life. Then he died, and I went to his funeral. Can you tell me why?

Actually, the two days before the ceremony were most interesting. The concierge's wife was ill, in bed in their one room, and the coffin had been placed near her on trestles. You had to collect your own mail. You opened the door and said: 'Good morning, Madame.' Then you would listen as she gestured towards the dear departed and sang his praises. Nothing too amusing about that, huh? Yet everyone in the building went into her room, which stank of carbolic. The tenants didn't send their servants, either: no, they came down to enjoy this golden opportunity for themselves. Of course, the servants came too, but on the sly. When the day came for the funeral, the coffin was too wide to go through the door of the lodge. 'Oh, the darling,' the concierge said from her bed, with a mixture of surprise, delight and distress. 'How big he was!' 'Don't worry, Madame,' the undertaker said. 'We'll take him through sideways and upright.' They took him through upright, then they laid him down again and I was the only person (apart from a former nightclub bouncer who apparently used to drink his Pernod every evening with the dead man) to go as far as the cemetery and throw some flowers on the coffin – which seemed to me a surprisingly expensive one. Finally, I paid the concierge's wife a visit, to accept her thanks, which were performed with tragic emotion. Tell me, what was that all about? Nothing, just an aperitif.

I also buried an old fellow member of the Bar Association, a clerk whom nobody really noticed, though I always used to shake his hand. Actually, I shook everyone's hand at work and usually more than once a day. This simple cordiality cost me little but gained everyone's sympathy, which was necessary for my enjoyment of life. The president of the Association didn't bother to turn up for the burial of our clerk, but I did – and it was the day before I had to go away somewhere, a fact that did not go unobserved. I knew that my presence would be noted and talked about with approval. So you can see that not even the snow that fell on the day made me hestitate.

What? I'm getting to it, don't worry. In fact, I'm there. But first let me point out that the concierge's wife, who had spent a fortune on crucifixes and fine oak and silver handles for the coffin, the better to enjoy her grief, took up a month later with a handsome swell with a good singing voice. He used to beat her, and you would hear these dreadful screams, immediately after which he would open the window and launch into his favourite ballad: 'Women, how pretty you are!' 'I ask you!' the neighbours would say. Ask you what? Admittedly, appearances were against the baritone, and the concierge as well; but there's no proof that they were not in love. There's no proof, either, that she did not love her husband. In any case, when the swell took off, after exhausting his voice and his right arm, the loyal widow resumed her eulogy of her dead husband! In any case, I know others, who have appearances on their side, who are not more faithful or more sincere. There was one man who gave twenty years of his life to a scatter-brained woman, sacrificing everything in his life for her – friends, work, even respectability – only to acknowledge one evening that he had never loved her. He was bored, that's all, bored, like most people; so he created from scratch a life of complications and drama for himself. Something's got to happen – that's the explanation for most human undertakings. Something's got to happen, even if it's slavery without love, or war, or death. So long live funerals!

I, at any rate, did not have that excuse. I was not bored, because I was in charge. On the evening in question, I might even say that I was less bored than ever. No, really, I didn't want anything to happen. And yet . . . You see, my dear sir, it was a lovely autumn evening, still warm in town, but already damp over the Seine. Night was falling, the sky was still light in the west, but getting darker, and the street lights shone weakly. I was walking along the *quais* on the Left Bank towards the Pont des Arts, looking at the gleam of the water in the spaces between the closed stalls of the second-hand booksellers. There were few people on the riverbank: Paris was already eating. My feet rustled through the yellow, dusty leaves which reminded one of summer. Bit by bit the sky was filling up with stars, which you could see briefly as you walked away from one street lamp and towards the next. I was enjoying the return of silence, the sweetness of the evening and Paris empty. I was happy. My day had been good: a blind man, the reduction in sentence that I had hoped for, a warm handshake from my client, a few generous gestures and, in the afternoon, a brilliant speech, improvised for a few friends, on the hardness of heart of our ruling classes and the hypocrisy of the elite.

I went up on to the Pont des Arts, which was deserted at that time, to watch the river, barely visible now that night had fallen. I was overlooking the Ile de la Cité and facing the Vert-Galant park. I felt rise up in me a great sense of power and – how shall I say? – of completeness that gladdened my heart. I drew myself up and lit a cigarette, the cigarette of satisfaction, when at the same moment, there was a burst of laughter behind me. I swung round in surprise, but there was no one there. I went up to the railing: no barges, no boats. I turned round to face the island again and once more heard the laughter behind me, a little further off, as though going down the river. I stayed there without moving. The laugh was getting fainter, but I could still hear it distinctly behind me, coming out of nowhere except the water. At the same time I noticed that my heart was beating faster. Let me be clear about this: there was nothing mysterious about the laughter, it was good laughter, natural and almost friendly, putting the world to rights. Besides which, I could very soon not hear it any more. I returned to the *quais*, went down the Rue Dauphine and bought some cigarettes that I didn't need. I was dazed and gasping for breath. That evening, I called a friend, who was not at home. I was thinking of going out when, suddenly, I heard a laugh outside the window. I opened it. Below on the street, some young people were saying cheerful goodbyes. I closed the window, shrugging my shoulders. Then I went into the bathroom to drink a glass of water. My face smiled back at me from the mirror, but it seemed to me that the smile was double . . .

What? Oh, excuse me, I was thinking of something else.

I expect I'll see you tomorrow. Yes, tomorrow, that's it. No, no, I can't stay. In any case, I'm due for a consultation with the brown bear you can see over there. A decent man, no doubt about it, who is being cruelly victimized by the police out of pure malice. You think he looks like a killer? Rest assured: looks do not deceive. He's also a pretty good burglar, and you might be surprised to learn that this caveman specializes as a dealer in pictures. In Holland, everyone is a specialist in paintings and tulips. This man, with his unassuming air, is responsible for the most famous of art thefts. Which one? I may tell you sometime. Don't be surprised by my expertise. Even though I'm a judge-penitent, I have a hobby here: I am the legal counsellor to these fine people. I have studied the laws of the country and picked up a clientele in this district, where they don't ask for your diplomas. It wasn't easy, but I inspire confidence, don't I? I have a fine, open laugh and a firm handshake: those are advantages. And then I dealt with some hard cases, firstly out of interest, then through conviction. If pimps and thieves were always universally condemned, then decent people would all consider themselves innocent the whole time, my dear sir. And in my opinion – all right, all right, I'm coming! – that's the chief thing we have to avoid. Otherwise it would just be a joke.

Honestly, my dear fellow, I do appreciate your curiosity. Yet there's nothing extraordinary about my story. I'll tell you, since you want to know, that I thought about the laugh a bit for a few days, then forgot it. Occasionally, it seemed as though I could hear it somewhere inside me. But, most of the time, I had no difficulty thinking about other things.

I must confess, though, that I didn't return to the banks of the Seine. When I did go past the *quais*, in a car or a bus, a kind of inner silence came over me. I think I was waiting. But I would cross the Seine, nothing would happen and I breathed again. At that time, I also had a few problems with my health. Nothing definite, I was run down if you like, and found it hard to recover my good spirits. I saw doctors and they gave me pick-me-ups. These picked me up, then I went down again. Life got harder for me: when the body is sad, the heart languishes. I felt as though I was partly unlearning what I had never learned and yet knew so well: I mean, how to live. Yes, I really think that this was when it all started.

But I'm not really feeling myself this evening, either. I'm even having trouble forming a sentence. I get the feeling that I'm not speaking fluently and I'm expressing myself less well. The weather, I expect. It's hard to breathe, and the air is so heavy that it weighs on my chest. My dear fellow, would you mind terribly if we were to go out and walk around town a little? Thank you.

How lovely the canals are in the evening! I like the breath of stagnant water, the smell of dead leaves steeped in moisture and the funerary odour that rises from barges full of flowers. No, no, believe me, there's nothing morbid in my liking for those things. On the contrary, it's a conscious decision for me: in truth, I force myself to admire the canals. What I love most in the world is Sicily, you understand, and most of all from the summit of Etna, in daylight, provided I can see the full extent of the island and the sea. Java, too, but when the trade winds are blowing. Yes, I went there when I was young. In general, I love all islands: it's easier to dominate them.

That's a charming house, isn't it? The two heads there belong to negro slaves. A trade sign: the owner was a slave-trader. Huh, they didn't mince their words in those days! They came right out with it and said: 'I've got a house on the street, I deal in slaves, I sell black flesh!' Can you imagine anyone nowadays stating publicly that that was his business? What an uproar! I could hear my fellow lawyers in Paris from here. They're adamant on this matter and wouldn't hesitate to publish two or three manifestos, maybe more! When I think about it, I might even add my signature to theirs. Slavery? Why, no, we're against it! If we are forced to have it in the home or in factories, fine, that's the normal run of things, but boasting about it, is going too far.

I'm well aware of the fact that one cannot do without dominating or being served. Every man needs slaves just as he needs fresh air. Giving orders is like breathing, you must agree? And even the most abject man manages to breathe. The lowest on the social ladder still has his wife or child. If he's unmarried, a dog. The main thing, when it comes down to it, is to be able to lose one's temper when the other can't answer back. 'You don't answer back to your father' – you've heard that one, I suppose? In a sense, it's an odd idea, because who would you answer back to, except someone you love? Yet, in another way, it's an effective argument. Someone has to have the last word. Otherwise every point of view would give rise to its opposite and there'd be no end to it all. Power, on the other hand, settles everything. It's taken us some time, but we've realized this at last. For example, you must have noticed that our old Europe is finally thinking along the right lines. We don't say any longer, as we used to in more innocent times: 'There's what I think. Now what are your objections?' We've reached the age of lucidity: dialogue has been replaced by communiqués. 'Here's the truth,' we say. 'You can argue over it if you wish, we don't care, but in a few years the police will come and show you I'm right.'

Oh, our dear planet! It's all clear now. We know ourselves, we know what we're capable of. Changing examples, but not the subject: take me, now: I always liked to be served with a smile. If the maid looked miserable, she ruined my day. Of course, she was quite entitled not to be happy, but I told myself that it was better for her to carry out her duties smiling rather than weeping. In reality, it was better for me. Yet my point of view, while nothing to boast about, was not entirely stupid. In the same way, I refused to eat in Chinese restaurants. Why? Because Orientals often look contemptuous when they are in the presence of Whites and not speaking. Of course, that's how they look when they serve you. And how can you enjoy a lacquered chicken – above all, how can you think you are in the right – in those circumstances?

Just between ourselves, servitude, preferably with a smile, is unavoidable. But we don't have to acknowledge that fact. If a man can't help having slaves, isn't it better for him to call them free men? As a matter of principle, firstly, then so as not to drive them to despair. Surely we owe them at least that compensation? In this way, they will carry on smiling and we can keep our conscience clean. Otherwise, we might be forced to examine ourselves and become mad with grief, or modest . . . Anything could happen. So: no trade signs and this one is outrageous. In any case, if everyone started doing it, I mean advertising his true business, what he really is, then we wouldn't know if we were coming or going! Just imagine visiting cards for: 'Dupont, cowardly philosopher', or 'Christian landlord'; or 'adulterous humanist' – there's no end to it, really. It would be hell! Yes, that's what hell must be like: streets with trade signs and no chance to explain oneself away. You would be pigeon-holed once and for all.

You, for example, my dear compatriot, just consider what your sign would be. You've nothing to say? Well, then, tell me later. In any case, I know mine: a double face, a charming Janus with, above it, the motto of the firm: 'Don't trust us'. On my visiting cards, 'Jean-Baptiste Clamence, actor'. Why, now, shortly after the evening I mentioned, I made a discovery. When I would leave a blind man on the pavement after I had helped him to cross, I used to raise my hat to him. Obviously, this gesture was not intended for him, since he couldn't see it. So who was I addressing? The audience. After the performance, the bow. Not bad, eh? On another occasion, at the same time, a driver was thanking me for giving him directions, and I replied that no one would have done as much. Of course, I meant 'anyone'. But I could not forget this wretched slip of the tongue. When it came to modesty, I was unbeatable.

My good fellow, I have to admit, with all humility, that I have always been supremely vain. Me, me, me: that's the refrain that runs through my precious life and you could hear it in everything I said. I have never been able to speak without boasting, especially if I did so with that resounding restraint that I was so good at.

It's true that I have always lived free and in control. Quite simply, I felt liberated in my relations with others for the excellent reason that I recognized no equal to myself. I have always considered myself more intelligent than anyone, as I told you, but also more sensitive and more skilled, a crack shot, a peerless driver, the best lover. Even in areas where I could easily recognize my inferiority, such as tennis, it was hard for me to believe that, if I had time to train, I should not outclass the top seeds. I saw only superiority in myself, which explained my benevolence and peace of mind. When I did care for another person, it was out of pure condescension, freely conceded, and all the merit was mine. I would rise by a degree on the scale of self-love.

Along with a few other truths, I discovered these facts gradually in the period following the evening I mentioned to you. Not all at once, certainly, or very clearly. First of all, I had to recover my memory. Bit by bit I saw more clearly and learned a little of what I knew. Up to that time, I had always been helped by an astonishing ability to forget. I forgot everything, starting with my resolutions. In the end, nothing counted: war, suicide, love, poverty – I paid attention to them, of course, when circumstances obliged me to do so, but in a formal, superficial way. Sometimes, I pretended to become deeply involved in a cause that had nothing to do with my everyday life; yet, when it came down to it, I did not participate, unless of course my own freedom was compromised. How shall I say? Everything slid . . . yes, everything slid over me.

To be fair, some of my forgetfulness was commendable. You will have noticed that there are people whose religion consists in forgiving all offences against them, and who do indeed forgive, but never forget. I was not up to forgiving offences, but I did eventually forget all of them – and a person who thought that I hated him would be amazed to see me greet him with a broad smile. Depending on his character, he would then either admire my generous soul or despise my faint-heartedness, never imagining that the reason was simpler: I had forgotten even as much as his name. So the same handicap that made me indifferent or ungrateful also made me magnanimous.

As a result, I lived from day to day with no continuity other than me-me-me. Women, from one day to the next, virtue or vice, from one day to the next, like a dog, from one day to the next, but every day myself, unmovable at my post. In this way, I proceeded across the surface of life in words, so to speak, never in reality. All those books hardly read, those friends hardly loved, those cities hardly visited and those women hardly possessed! I went through the motions, out of boredom or absent-mindedness. Other creatures followed behind, wanting to cling on, but there was nothing there – that was the trouble. For them. As for me, I forgot. The only thing I ever remembered was myself.

However, little by little, my memory came back. Or, rather, I went back to it and found the memories that were awaiting me. Before I tell you about them, let me give you a few examples, my dear fellow – which I'm sure will be of use to you – of things that I discovered in the course of my explorations.

One day, when I was driving my car and hesitated a moment before driving off at a green light, while our patient fellow citizens instantly started to sound their horns behind me, I suddenly recalled another episode that had taken place in similar circumstances. A motorcycle ridden by a thin little man with pince-nez and plus-fours overtook me and halted in front of me at the traffic lights. As he stopped, the man stalled his engine and was fruitlessly trying to restart it. When the lights changed, I asked him, with my accustomed good manners, to move his bike over so that I could get by. The little chap was getting still more annoyed about his wheezy engine and so told me, in accordance with the rules of Parisian etiquette, to get stuffed. I insisted, still politely, but with an edge of impatience in my tone. He immediately came back with the assurance that, in any case, I could comprehensively screw myself. Meanwhile, a few horns were starting to sound behind me. More firmly now I asked the man not to be rude and to consider that he was holding up the traffic. The irascible fellow, no doubt driven to a frenzy by the now evident recalcitrance of his engine, informed me that if I wanted what he called a good hammering, he would be delighted to give me one. This cynical attitude filled me with righteous anger and I got out of my car with the intention of boxing this foul-mouthed gentleman's ears. I don't think I'm a coward (though what doesn't one think?), I was a good head taller than my adversary and my muscles have always served me well. I still think that his hammering would have been received rather than given. But no sooner was I on the pavement than, out of the crowd that was gathering, a man emerged, rushed towards me, told me I was the most despicable creature and that he would not allow me to strike a man who was seated on a motorcycle and consequently at a disadvantage. I confronted this musketeer and, to tell the truth, I didn't actually see him. Hardly had I turned my head than, almost simultaneously, I heard the motorcycle splutter again and received a violent blow on the ear. Before I had time to register what had happened, the motorcycle was driving away. Stunned, I was walking mechanically towards d'Artagnan when, at the same second, a concerto of exasperated horns rose from the line of traffic which by this time had become quite long. The lights turned to green. At this, still slightly bewildered, instead of giving a good hiding to the idiot who had distracted my attention, I went tamely back to my car and turned on the engine while, as I walked past, the same idiot greeted me with the words 'you pathetic creature', which I can still hear.

A trivial incident, you may think. Of course. I merely took a long time to forget it: that's what is important. However, I did have an excuse. I had let myself be hit without hitting back, but no one could accuse me of cowardice. Taken by surprise, with people shouting at me from two directions, I was bewildered, and the horns completed my confusion. Yet I was as upset about it as if I had done something dishonourable. I kept seeing myself, getting into my car without sticking up for myself, with the sneering looks of a crowd that was all the more delighted, I remember, because I was wearing a very elegant blue suit. I heard that 'pathetic creature' and, in spite of everything, it seemed to me justified. The fact was I had climbed down in public – true, it was as a result of a combination of circumstances, but there are always circumstances. After the event, I saw clearly what I should have done. I imagined myself felling d'Artagnan with a right hook, getting back in my car and chasing after the swine who had hit me, catching up with him, blocking his cycle in against the pavement and delivering the beating that he so richly deserved. I ran this little film a hundred times, with odd variations, in my imagination. But it was too late and for a few days I would suffer from a feeling of bitter resentment.

Look at that, it's raining again. Let's stop, shall we, under this porch? Good. What was I saying? Oh, yes: honour. Well, when I recalled that incident, I realized what it meant. In short, my dream had not withstood the test of reality. It was now clear that I had dreamed of being a whole man who would be respected personally as well as professionally: half Cerdan, half de Gaulle, if you like. In short, I wanted to be dominant in every sphere. That's why I put on airs and took a pride in showing my physical prowess rather than my intellectual gifts. But after having been struck in public without striking back, it was no longer possible for me to nurture this fine image of myself. If I had really been the friend of truth and intellect that I claimed to be, what could that episode, already forgotten by those who had witnessed it, have meant to me? I would scarcely even have blamed myself for getting angry over nothing, and also, once I was angry, for not facing up to the consequences of my anger through a lack of presence of mind. Instead of that though, I was aching to get my revenge, to strike and win. As though my true desire was not to be the most intelligent and generous creature on earth, but merely to defeat whomsoever I wished, in short to be the strongest – and, moreover, in the most basic way. The truth is that every intelligent man, as you know, dreams of being a gangster and ruling over society by violence alone. As this is not as easy as one might think from reading novels in the genre, people generally turn to politics and hurry to support the cruellest party. It matters little, wouldn't you say, to abase one's mind if by that means one succeeds in dominating everyone. I found that there were sweet dreams of oppression within me.

I did at least learn that I was on the side of the guilty – the defendants – only to the precise extent that their crime did not cause any harm to me. Their culpability made me eloquent because I was not the victim. When I was threatened, I became not only a judge like the rest, but more than that: an angry master who wanted to strike the wrongdoer and bring him to his knees, regardless of any law. After that, my dear fellow, it is hard to go on seriously believing that one has a vocation to do justice and that one is the preordained defender of the widow and the orphan.

Since the rain is falling more heavily and we have some time, might I venture to confide another discovery to you, one that I made soon after, as I remember it? Let's sit out of the rain on this bench. For centuries, pipe smokers have been staring at this same rain falling over that same canal. What I have to tell you is rather more difficult. This time, a woman is involved. First of all, you must know that I have always been a success with women, without trying too hard. I'm not saying that I have managed to make them happy, or even to make myself happy through them; no, just success. I reached my goal, more or less whenever I wanted. I was considered charming, if you can believe that! You know what charm is: a way of obtaining the answer 'yes' without having asked a clear question. So it was with me, at that time. Are you surprised? Come on, don't deny it. It's quite normal, with me looking the way I do now. Alas, after a certain age every man is responsible for his face! Mine . . . But what does it matter! The fact remains that I was considered attractive and I made the most of it.

It was not at all calculating: I was sincere, or almost. My relationship with women was natural, straightforward, uncomplicated as they say. There was no deception involved, or merely that blatant deception that they consider a mark of respect. As people commonly say, I loved women – which amounts to saying that I never loved any one of them. I have always thought misogyny to be both vulgar and stupid, and considered almost all the women I have known to be better than myself. However, while setting them so high, I exploited rather than served them. What does that mean?

Of course, true love is the exception: roughly two or three instances a century. The rest of the time, it's a case of vanity or boredom. In any case, where I was concerned, I was no Portuguese nun. I am not cold-hearted, far from it, in fact I am full of tenderness and I cry easily. However, my emotional impulses always turn inwards, towards myself, and I am the one I pity. It is wrong, after all, to say that I have never loved. In my life, I have had at least one great love, always with myself as its object. From that point of view, after the inevitable difficulties of extreme youth, I settled early on one thing: sensuality alone governed my love life. I looked solely for objects of pleasure and conquest. Moreover, I was helped in this by my looks: nature had been generous to me. I was not a little proud of the fact and got a great deal of satisfaction from it, though I cannot tell if it was a matter of pleasure or prestige. There, you'll be telling me that I'm boasting again. I won't deny it and I am still less proud of the fact since in this case I am boasting of something true.

In any event, my sensuality (speaking only of that) was so genuine that, even for a ten-minute adventure, I would have denied my father and mother, even if that meant bitterly regretting it. What am I saying! *Especially* for a ten-minute adventure and still more so if I could be sure that it would end there. I did have principles, of course, one of which, for example, was that my friends' wives were sacred. It was just that, quite sincerely, I would stop being friends with the husbands a few days in advance. Perhaps sensuality is not the right word. After all, sensuality is not repulsive. Let's be kind and use the word 'infirmity' – a sort of congenital incapacity for seeing love as anything other than making love. After all, it was a comfortable infirmity. Combined with my power of forgetting, it gave me more freedom; and, at the same time, by imbuing me with a certain distance and a sense of irreducible independence, it led me on to further conquests. By not being romantic, I nourished romantic ideas in others, because our women friends have one thing in common with Bonaparte, which is that they always think they will succeed where others have failed.

In our dealings, moreover, I would satisfy something else, in addition to my sensuality: my love of playacting. I loved women as partners in a kind of game which did, at least, have a feeling of innocence. You see, I can't stand being bored, and the only thing I really enjoy in life is entertainment. Any company, however brilliant, soon overwhelms me, while I have never been bored with women I desired. It is hard to admit, but I should have exchanged ten meetings with Einstein for a first encounter with a pretty chorus girl. True, after the tenth encounter with her, I would be sighing for Einstein or a serious book. In short, I have never bothered about weighty matters except in the intervals between my little excesses. I can't think how many times, standing on the pavement in the midst of a heated debate with some friends, I have lost the thread of the argument because a real smasher was crossing the street at that moment.

So I played the game. I knew that they did not like one to get to the point too soon. First, there had to be conversation and some tenderness, as they say. I was not short of things to say, being a lawyer, or of doting looks, since I had done some amateur dramatics during my military service. I often changed parts, but the play was always the same. For example, the scene of inexplicable attraction, that 'certain feeling', that 'I can't explain it, I wasn't expecting to feel like this, actually I was weary of love, etc.': that always worked, though it's one of the oldest in the repertory. There was also the one about the mysterious love that no other woman has ever given you, a love that may be doomed to end (certainly is, in fact: you can't have too much insurance), but which, for that very reason, is unique. Most of all, I had perfected a little speech which was always a success and which I'm sure you will applaud. The heart of it lay in the painful and resigned assertion that I was nothing, it was not worthy becoming attached to me, my life was somewhere else and not connected with ordinary happiness, though I might well have preferred that kind of happiness to anything else, but, alas, it was too late. I kept quiet about the reasons for this crucial lateness, knowing that it is better to go to bed with a mystery. What's more, in a sense, I believed what I was saying: I lived my part, so it's not surprising that my partners, too, started to act their roles. The most sensitive of them tried to understand me and this effort created a sort of melancholy abandonment in them. The rest, happy to see that I was playing the game according to the rules and having the decency to speak before I acted, moved on to the point of it all without delay. So I had won, indeed, doubly so because, apart from the desire that I felt for them, I was satisfying my love for myself by proving my exceptional abilities on every occasion.

So true is this that even when some of them provided me with only a small degree of pleasure, I still tried to resume our relations from time to time, helped no doubt by that peculiar desire which is stimulated by absence, followed by a suddenly rediscovered intimacy; but also to make sure that the bond between us was still there and that it was up to me alone to revive it. Sometimes, I would even go so far as to make them swear that they would not belong to any other man, in order to set my mind at rest on that point once and for all. Yet such anxieties did not affect my heart or even my imagination. Indeed, I so exactly personified a particular kind of conceit that it was hard for me to imagine, despite evidence to the contrary, that a woman who had been mine could ever belong to another man. But by swearing, they freed me while binding themselves. Once they would not be anyone else's, I could bring myself to break with them – something that, otherwise, it was almost always impossible for me to do. Where they were concerned, I had the proof I needed once and for all, and my power was assured for a long time. Odd, isn't it? Yet that's how it is, my dear chap. Some people shout: 'Love me!' Others: 'Don't love me!' But there is a group, the worst and most miserable, who say: 'Don't love me, but be faithful!'

The trouble is, though, that the proof is never definite; you have to start afresh with each new person. And, by starting again, you pick up habits. Soon the lines come to you without thinking and the reflex follows until one day you find yourself in the position of taking without really desiring. At least for some people, believe me, not taking what you don't want is the hardest thing in the world.

That is what happened one day. There is no point in telling you who she was, except to say that, without really arousing me, she had attracted me with her passive, eager manner. Quite honestly, it was not up to much, as expected, but I've never had any complexes about failure and I soon forgot the woman, whom I didn't see again. I thought that she hadn't noticed anything; it didn't even cross my mind that she could have an opinion. In any case, as far as I was concerned, her passivity cut her off from the world. Yet a few weeks later I learned that she had told a third party about my inadequacy. Immediately, I felt as though I had been deceived in some way: she hadn't been as passive as I believed; she had a mind of her own. Then I shrugged my shoulders and pretended to laugh. In fact, I really did laugh: obviously the incident was trivial. If there is one area in which modesty ought to be the rule, surely it's sex, with all its unpredictability. But no, we rival each other in who will make the best show, even when we're alone. I shrugged my shoulders, but what did I actually do? I saw the woman again, shortly afterwards, I did what was needed to seduce her properly and really win her back. It wasn't very hard: women, too, don't like an affair to end in failure. From then on, without really wanting to, I started to mortify her in every way. I gave her up, then took her back, I obliged her to make love at inappropriate times and places, and treated her in such a brutal manner, in every respect, that eventually I became attached to her as I imagine a jailer is bound to his prisoner. This continued until the day when, in the violent throes of a pleasure that was both painful and imposed, she acknowledged aloud her appreciation of the thing that was enslaving her. From that day on, I began to separate from her and since that, I have forgotten her.

I must agree with you, despite your polite silence, that this adventure was not very edifying. But think about your own life, my dear fellow! Dig into your memory and you may perhaps find a similar story that you will tell me later. As for me, when I happened to recall that affair, I still had to laugh. But it was a different laugh, not unlike the one I heard on the Pont des Arts. I was laughing at my speeches and my pleas in court. More at my pleas, in fact, than at my speeches to women. At least, I did not lie to them. Instinct spoke clearly, without prevarication, in my attitude. For example, the act of love is a confession. It cries out, blatantly, with egotism, or vanity is clearly displayed, or else it reveals true generosity. Finally, in this unfortunate story more than in my other affairs, I was more open and honest than I imagined: I had stated who I was and how I could live. So, despite appearances, I was a more decent person in my private life even – and above all – when I was behaving as I have described, than in my great, lyrical outpourings on innocence and justice in court. At least, when I saw how I acted towards other people, I could not disguise the truth about my character from myself. No man is a hypocrite in his pleasures. Now, did I read that somewhere, my dear fellow, or did I think it?

So when I considered how hard it was for me finally to break up with a woman (something that resulted in my conducting so many affairs at the same time), I did not ascribe it to the softness of my heart. That is not what impelled me to act when one of my girlfriends wearied of waiting for the Austerlitz of our passion and spoke of ending it. I was the one who immediately took a step forward, made concessions and persuasive speeches. Tenderness and the sweetness of a soft heart were what I inspired in them;

I myself experienced only the shadow of these emotions, merely becoming a little agitated by this rejection and also alarmed by the possibility of losing affection. Sometimes, admittedly, I believed that I was truly suffering, yet the rebel needed only to leave me for real and I would have no trouble at all in forgetting her, just as I forgot her in my presence when, on the contrary, she had decided to come back. No, it was not love or generosity that spurred me on when I was in danger of being abandoned, but solely the desire to be loved and to receive what I considered my due. Once I was loved and my partner had once more been forgotten, I shone again, I was at my best, I was pleasant to be with.

You should note that, as soon as I had recovered this affection, it would weigh on me. Then, in my moments of irritation, I would tell myself that the ideal solution would have been the death of the person concerned. Death would, on the one hand, have consolidated our bond once and for all, while on the other removing its constraints. But one cannot desire the death of everyone or wish, at the extreme, to depopulate the planet in order to enjoy a freedom that would be unimaginable otherwise. That would be incompatible with my sensibility and my love of mankind.

The only profound emotion that I sometimes felt in these affairs was gratitude, when everything was going well and I was granted, as well as peace of mind, the freedom to come and go: never was I gentler or happier with one of them than when I had just left the bed of another, as though I were extending the debt that I had incurred with one woman to all of them. Besides, whatever might have been the apparent confusion of my feelings, the result for me was clear: I kept all my affections going around me, in order to use them when I wished. So, by my own admission, I could not live unless all creatures throughout the world, or the greatest possible number, were turned towards me, eternally vacant, deprived of independent life, ready to respond to my call at any moment, in short, condemned to sterility until the day when I might deign to shine my light upon them. In short, for me to live happily, all the creatures whom I chose had not to live at all. They were only to receive life, from time to time, at my good pleasure.

Oh, believe me, I feel no satisfaction in telling you this. If I think of that period when I demanded everything without paying and when I mobilized so many creatures to serve me, putting them as it were in cold storage so that they could be available one day or another, at my convenience, I am not sure what to call the odd feeling that comes over me. Could it be shame? Tell me, my good friend, doesn't shame burn a little? Yes? Then it may be shame or one of those ridiculous feelings connected with honour. In any case, I get the impression that this feeling has not left me since the episode that is at the heart of my memory and which I shall soon have to describe to you, in spite of my digressions and other inventive efforts for which, I hope, you are giving me credit.

Look, the rain's stopped! Please be good enough to accompany me home. I am tired, oddly, not from talking, but at the sole idea of what I have still to say. Come, now! A few words will be enough to describe my crucial discovery. Indeed, why say more? For the statue to be naked, one must strip away all the fine words. So. That particular night, in November, two or three years before the evening when I thought I heard a laugh behind my back, I was going to the Left Bank and home across the Pont Royal. It was an hour past midnight and a light rain was falling, more like a drizzle, which scattered the few passers-by. I had just left a mistress who must surely have been still asleep. I was pleased with the walk, a little numb, and my body was calm, rinsed by blood as soft and sweet as the falling rain. On the bridge, I passed behind a figure leaning over the parapet and apparently looking down at the river. Getting closer, I could make out a slender young woman, dressed in black. All that could be seen of her between the dark hair and the collar of her coat was the back of her neck, fresh and damp, which I found touching. But, after a moment's hesitation, I continued on my way. Reaching the end of the bridge, I turned along the *quai* towards Saint-Michel, where I was then living. I had already gone some fifty metres when I heard the sound – a sound which, despite the distance, seemed immense in the silence of the night – of a body hitting the water. I stopped dead, but without turning round. Almost at once, I heard a shout, repeated several times, which was also travelling down the river, then abruptly stopped. The ensuing silence seemed interminable, as though the night had stopped dead. I wanted to run, but couldn't move. I was trembling, I think, with cold and shock. I told myself that I had to act quickly, but I felt an irresistible weakness flood through my body. I forget what I thought at that moment. 'Too late, too far away . . .', or something like that. I kept on listening, not moving. Then, slowly, I walked away through the rain. I reported the incident to no one.

Here we are: this is my house, my refuge. Tomorrow? Yes, if you will. I'd like to take you to the island of Marken and you could see the Zuyder Zee. We'll meet at eleven at Mexico City. What? The woman? I can't really tell you, I don't know. The next day, and those that followed, I didn't read the newspapers.

A toytown village, don't you think? They didn't go easy on the picturesque here! But I didn't bring you to this island to enjoy the local colour, my dear chap. Anyone could show you the headdresses, clogs and multi-coloured houses where fishermen smoke their pipes in an aura of beeswax. On the contrary: I am one of the few people who can show you what is important here.

We are getting near the dyke. We have to go along it to get as far as possible away from those excessively pretty houses. Please have a seat. What do you think? There, isn't that the finest of negative landscapes? Look, on the left we have that pile of ashes that they call a dune here, with the grey dyke on our right, the pallid beach at our feet and, in front of us, the sea, the colour of diluted washing powder, its pale waters reflected in the vast sky above. A soft hell, it really is! Nothing but horizontals, no brightness: colourless space and dead life. Is it not universal obliteration, a void perceptible to the eyes? No men, above all, no men! Just you and I, only us, face-to-face with a planet that is finally empty. The sky is alive? You're right, dear friend. It thickens, then sinks back, opens up airy staircases, then closes its doors of cloud. Those are doves. Have you noticed that the Dutch sky is full of millions of doves, so high up that they are invisible, which flap their wings, rising and falling as one, filling the celestial dome with thick clouds of greyish feathers that the wind carries away or brings back. The doves wait up there, they wait all year round. They circle above the earth, looking, wanting to come down. But there is nothing, only the sea and the canals, roofs covered with signs and no head on which to land.

You don't understand what I mean? I must confess that I'm tired. I lose the thread of what I'm saying; I no longer have that clarity of mind on which my friends used to compliment me. I say 'my friends', by the way, as a manner of speaking. I have no friends any more, only accomplices. On the other hand, the number of those has grown: they are the whole human race, with you in first place. The person who is here is always first. How do I know that I don't have any friends? Very simple: I found out on the day when I considered killing myself in order to play a trick on them – to punish them in a way. But to punish whom? Some people would be surprised, but no one would feel punished. I realized that I had no friends. In any case, suppose I had had any: it wouldn't have got me anywhere. If I might have been able to commit suicide and then see the effect on them, why, yes, it could have been worth it. But earth is dark, dear friend, and wood is thick, and a shroud is opaque. Yes, of course, there are the eyes of the soul – if there is a soul and it has eyes! But, there you are, one cannot be sure, one is never sure. Otherwise, there would be a solution and one could at last be taken seriously. Men are not convinced of your arguments, your sincerity or the seriousness of your suffering, except by your death. As long as you are alive, your case is debatable and you only deserve their scepticism. Then, if there was the slightest certainty that one could enjoy the sight of it, it might be worth proving what they do not want to believe and giving them a shock. But you kill yourself, and it doesn't matter whether or not they believe you: you are not there to witness their astonishment and their contrition (short-lived, anyway), or to take part in your

46

own funeral, as every man dreams of doing. If we are to end, doubt, we must stop existing, purely and simply.

In any case, isn't it better that way? We should suffer too much from their indifference. 'You'll pay for it!' a young girl said to her father who had prevented her from marrying a suitor who was too well turned out. And she killed herself. But the father didn't pay a thing. He loved fly-fishing. Three Sundays later, he went back to the river – to forget, or so he said. He had guessed right: he did forget. Quite honestly, the contrary would have been surprising. A person thinks he is dying to punish his wife, and he gives her back her freedom. Better not to see that. Quite apart from the fact that you might hear the reasons that they give for what you did: in my case, I can hear them already: 'He killed himself because he could not bear to . . .' Oh, my good friend, how feeble is the imagination of men. They always think that people commit suicide for a reason. But one can very well commit suicide for two reasons. No, that idea doesn't enter their heads. So what's the use of dying voluntarily and sacrificing oneself to the idea that you want to give of yourself? Once you're dead, they'll take the opportunity to assign idiotic or vulgar motives to your action. My dear friend, martyrs should choose to be forgotten, mocked or exploited. As for being understood, never.

Well, let's go straight to the point: I like life, that's my real weakness. I like it so much that I have no imagination when it comes to what is not it. There's something plebeian about such avidity, don't you think? The aristocracy doesn't conceive of itself without a certain distance towards itself and its own life. If necessary, one dies, and one breaks rather than bend. But I bend, because I continue to love myself. Well, now, after everything I've told you, what do you think I experienced? Disgust with myself? Come, come, if I was disgusted, it was chiefly with other people. I grant you, I knew my weaknesses and was sorry for them. But I went on forgetting them, with an almost commend-able obstinacy, while in my heart I never ceased to judge others. Surely, you must be shocked by that? Perhaps you think it's illogical? But it's not a matter of remaining logical. The matter is to slip past and above all – oh, yes, above all! – it's a matter of not being judged. I don't say of avoiding punishment, because punishment without judgement is bearable. Actually, it has a name which ensures our innocence: we call it 'misfortune'. No, on the contrary, it's a question of curtailing judgement, of escaping always being judged, without the sentence ever being pronounced.

However, you don't curtail it so easily. We are always ready for judgement nowadays, as for fornication – with the difference that you have no need to worry about not coming up to scratch. If you don't believe me, listen to the conversation around the table in August at those holiday hotels where our generous fellow countrymen take their boredom cure. If you're still not convinced, read the writings of the great men of the moment. Or watch your own family: you'll learn something. My dear friend, we mustn't give them even the slightest excuse to judge us! Otherwise, we end up in pieces. We have to take the same sort of precautions as a lion-tamer. If he has the misfortune, before going into the cage, to cut himself while shaving, what a feast for the creatures! I realized that all at once, on the day when the suspicion arrived that, perhaps, I was not such an admirable man. Since then, I have become wary. If I bled a little, then all was lost: they would devour me.

My relations with my contemporaries were apparently unchanged, yet they became subtly off-key. My friends hadn't changed. They still, from time to time, spoke warmly about the harmony and security that they found in being with me. But I could only detect the disharmonies and the disorder that filled me; I felt vulnerable and open to public accusation. My peers ceased to be in my eyes the respectful audience to which I was accustomed. The circle that had formed around me was broken and they were lined up in a single row, as if in a courtroom. In short, the moment that I perceived that there was something to be judged in me, I realized that they had an irresistible urge to judge. Yes, they were there, as before, but they were laughing. Or rather it seemed to me that each of those I met was looking at me with a hidden smile. I even had the impression, at that time, that people were tripping me up. And I did indeed stumble two or three times, for no reason, as I was entering a public place. Once I even fell over completely. Being a Cartesian Frenchman, I speedily recovered and ascribed these incidents to the only reasonable divinity, by which I mean chance. Even so, I remained suspicious.

Once I was alerted, it was not hard for me to discover that I had enemies: in my work, first of all, then in my social life. Some I had obliged, others I should have obliged. In short, all was as you would expect, and the discovery didn't cause me too much grief. On the other hand, it was harder and more painful for me to accept that I had enemies among those whom I knew very little, or not at all. I had always thought – you have already seen some evidence of my naivety – that people who did not know me could not help liking me if we did happen to meet. Well, no! I found animosity most of all among those who knew me only from afar while I myself did not know them at all. No doubt they suspected that I lived a full life, devoted to pleasure alone: that is unforgivable. An aura of success, when it is worn in a certain way, would drive a donkey to distraction. Then again, my life was full to bursting, and I refused many offers through lack of time. Afterwards, for the same reason, I would forget my refusals. But the offers had been made to me by people whose lives were not full and who, for that very reason, remembered my refusals.

This, to take just one example, is why in the end women cost me a lot. The time that I spent with them was time that I could not give to men, who did not always forgive me for it. What's the solution? You are only excused for happiness and success if you generously agree to share them. But if one is to be happy, one should not worry too much about other people – which means that there is no way out. Happy and judged or absolved and miserable. In my case, the injustice was even greater: I was condemned for past happiness. I had long lived under the illusion of universal accord, while in reality criticism, jibes and scorn rained down upon me, and I remained smiling and oblivious. As soon as I became aware of it, lucidity arrived. I received all the wounds at once and lost my strength at a single blow. Then the whole universe began to laugh around me.

That is something that no man – apart from someone who does not live, I mean a sage – can abide. The only thing on show is spite, so people hasten to judge, so as to avoid being judged themselves. What do you expect? The most natural idea for mankind, the one that comes naively, as if from the depths of one's being, is that of one's own innocence. In this respect we are all like the little Frenchman in Buchenwald who insisted on trying to lodge an appeal through the clerk, himself a prisoner, who had registered his arrival. The clerk and his friends laughed: 'Useless, old chap. There's no appeal here.' 'But, you see, Monsieur,' said the little Frenchman, 'mine is an exceptional case: I'm innocent!'

We are all exceptional cases; we all want to appeal over something! Each of us demands to be innocent, at any price, even if our being so means accusing the human race and heaven. You will give a man only slight pleasure if you compliment him on the efforts through which he has become intelligent or generous, while on the contrary his face will light up if you admire his natural generosity. On the other hand, if you tell a criminal that his crime is not imputable to his nature or his character but to unfortunate circumstances, then he will be fiercely grateful to you. During your final address, he will even choose this moment to cry. Yet there is no merit in being born honest or intelligent, just as one is surely no more responsible for being a criminal by nature than for being so through circumstances. But these rogues want pardon, that is to say irresponsibility; and they shamelessly plead justifications from nature or excuses from circumstances, even if these are contradictory. The main thing is for them to be innocent: that their virtues, by the divine grace of birth, cannot be challenged, and that their faults, the product of a passing misfortune, can only ever be temporary. As I told you, it's a question of escaping judgement. Since this is hard to do, a difficult business of getting people at once to admire and excuse your nature, they all try to be rich. Why? Is that what you were wondering? For the power, of course. But above all because wealth shields from immediate judgement, lifts you out of the crowd in the underground, shuts you up in a chromium-plated car and isolates you in huge expanses of protected parkland, or sleeping-cars and luxury cabins. Wealth, my dear friend, is not actually acquittal, but a reprieve – always worth having . . .

Most of all, don't believe your friends when they ask you to be sincere with them. All they want is for you to sustain them in the good opinion that they have of themselves and provide them with the additional assurance that they take from your promise of sincerity. How could sincerity be a condition of friendship? A liking for the truth at all costs is a passion that spares nothing and that nothing can withstand. It's a vice, sometimes a comfort, or a form of selfishness. So if you find yourself in that situation, don't hesitate: promise to be truthful and lie as best you can. You will satisfy their deep desire and doubly prove your affection for them.

So much so that we rarely confide in those who are better than we are; rather, we avoid their company. Most of the time, on the contrary, we confess to those who are like us and who share our weaknesses. This means that we do not want to correct ourselves or to be improved: for that, first of all, we should have to be judged and found wanting. All we need is to be pitied and encouraged in our course. In short, we would like at the same time to be no longer guilty and not to make the effort to purify ourselves. Not enough cynicism, not enough virtue. We have neither the energy of evil nor that of good. Do you know Dante? Really? The devil you do. So you will know that Dante allows for neutral angels in the quarrel between God and Satan; and he places them in Limbo, a sort of waiting-room for his Hell. My good friend, we're in the waiting-room.

Patience? No doubt you're right. We should have the patience to await the last judgement. But, there it is: we're in a hurry – to the point where I was obliged to become a judge-penitent. However, before that I had to come to terms with what I had discovered and make peace with the laughter of my contemporaries. From the evening when I heard the call – because I was truly called – I had to answer or at least seek the answer. It was not easy: I wandered around for a long time. First of all that perpetual laughter, and the people who were laughing, had to teach me to see more clearly within myself and to discover finally that I was not simple. Don't smile, that truth is not as elementary as it seems. What we call elementary truths are the ones that we discover after the rest, that's all.

However that may be, in the course of an extensive study of myself, I have laid bare the duplicity of the human animal. By searching through my memory, I realized that modesty helped me to shine, humility to triumph and virtue to oppress. I made war by peaceful means and in the end obtained all that I desired through unselfishness. For example, I never complained if people forgot the date of my birthday; they even expressed surprise, with a hint of admiration, at my reticence on this subject. But I was even more reticent about the reason for my unselfishness: I wished to be forgotten so that I could feel sorry for myself. Some days before the day, glorious among all others, the date of which I knew very well, I would be on the alert, careful not to let anything out that might stir the attention and the memory of those on whose oversight I was counting – didn't I even think on one occasion of altering someone's calendar? When my solitude had been clearly demonstrated, I could give myself up to the charms of virile melancholy.

In this way, the face of all my virtues had a less imposing obverse. It is true that, in another sense, all my faults turned to my advantage. For example, being obliged to conceal the depravity in my life gave me a cold manner which was confused with a virtuous one, my indifference won me love and my selfishness ended in acts of generosity. I must stop: too much symmetry would damage the argument. Why! I appeared hard, yet I have never been able to resist the offer of a drink or a woman! I was considered active and energetic, yet my kingdom was the bed. I proclaimed my loyalty, yet I think that there is not a single person that I loved whom I did not also eventually betray. Of course, my betrayals did not get in the way of my fidelity, I did achieve a considerable amount of work by means of sheer idleness and I never ceased to help my fellow creatures, because of the pleasure that this gave me. But, however much I repeated these evident truths, I got only little consolation from them. Some mornings, I would conduct my trial to the very end and reach the conclusion that what I excelled in above all was contempt. The very people that I most often helped were those I most despised. With courtesy and a deeply felt sense of solidarity, I daily spat in the faces of the blind.

Frankly, is there any excuse for this? There is one, but it is so feeble that I can't imagine using it. In any case, here it is: I have never been able to believe, deep inside, that human affairs are serious matters. I had no idea what was serious, only that it was not in everything that I saw, which seemed to me merely an amusing, or tedious game. There really are some efforts and beliefs that I have never understood. I would always look with astonishment, and some suspicion, on those strange creatures who died for money or were thrown into despair at the loss of a 'situation' or who sacrificed themselves with a great deal of show for the prosperity of their families. I could better understand one of my friends who decided to give up smoking and succeeded through sheer willpower. One morning, he opened the paper, read that the first hydrogen bomb had exploded, learned its admirable effects and went directly to a tobacconist's.

Of course, I did sometimes pretend to be taking life seriously. But the frivolity of seriousness itself very quickly became apparent to me and I merely continued to play my role as best I could. I played at being efficient, intelligent, righteous, a concerned citizen, indignant, indulgent, supportive, a good example ... In short, I need not continue: you have already realized that I was like these Dutchmen of mine who are here without being here: I was absent at the time when I occupied the most space. I have never truly been sincere and enthusiastic except when I used to play sports and, in the army, when I took part in the plays that we put on for our own enjoyment. In both cases, there was a set of rules, which was not serious, though you pretended to take it seriously. Even today, Sunday football matches in a crowded stadium, and the theatre, which I have loved with a unique passion, are the only places where I feel innocent.

But who would accept that such an attitude is permissible when it is a question of love, death or the wages of the poor? Yet what could be done? I could only imagine the love of Iseult in a novel or on the stage. The dying sometimes seemed to me to be playing their part with conviction. The words spoken by my poor clients always seemed to follow the same pattern. Thus, living among human beings without sharing their interests, I never managed to believe in the commitments I made. I was polite enough and lazy enough to meet expectations of me in my work, my family or my civic life, but every time with a sort of absent-mindedness that eventually spoiled everything. I spent my whole life under a dual sign and my most weighty actions were often those in which I was least involved. Wasn't this, after all, the thing that I could not forgive myself? And wasn't it this, just to add to my folly, that made me react most violently against the judgement that I felt at work in me and around me, forcing me to seek a way out?

For some time, in appearance, my life went on as though nothing had changed. I carried on along the same track. As if on purpose, the chorus of praise around me grew louder. In fact, that was the cause of the trouble. You remember: 'Woe betide you when all men speak well of you!' Ah, the person who said that was a wise one! Woe betide me! So the machine started to malfunction, to stop inexplicably.

It was at that moment that the idea of death encroached on my daily life. I measured the years that separated me from my end. I looked out for examples of men of my age who were dead already. And I was tormented by the idea that I might not have time to accomplish my task. What task? I didn't know. Quite honestly, was it worth going on with what I was doing? But this was not exactly the point. In fact I was pursued by a ridiculous fear: one could not die without having confessed all one's lies. Not to God or to one of his representatives: I was above that, as you might imagine. No, it was a matter of confessing to mankind, for example, to a friend or to a woman I loved. Otherwise, if there was only a single lie that remained hidden in a life, death would make it absolute. No one, ever again, would know the truth on that point because the only person to know it was the dead man, who had taken his secret with him. This absolute murder of a truth made my head swim. Today, incidentally, it would tend rather to give me exquisite pleasure. For example, the idea that I alone know what everyone is looking for and that I have at home an object that has kept the police forces of three countries occupied in vain is quite delicious. But, enough of that. At the time, I had not found the recipe and I was in torment.

Of course, I shook myself out of it. What did the lie of one man matter in the history of generations? How conceited was it to want to bring into the light of truth a miserable little deceit, lost in the ocean of the ages like a grain of salt in the sea! I also told myself that the death of the body, judging by those that I had seen, was punishment enough in itself and one that would absolve everything. One gained salvation (that is, the right to disappear once and for all) through the sweat of the death agony. No matter, my unease grew and death was a constant companion at my bedside: I would get up with it, and compliments became more and more unbearable to me. It seemed to me that the lie grew with them, to such an excessive extent that I could never again set things right.

The day came when I could stand it no longer. My first reaction was wild and confused. Since I was a liar, I would demonstrate the fact and throw my duplicity in the face of all those idiots before they even discovered it. As I was incited to tell the truth, I would take up the challenge. So, to anticipate mockery, I imagined casting myself into general derision. In short, this was another attempt to forestall judgement. I wanted to get the mockers on my side or, at least, to put myself on theirs. For example, I considered bumping into blind people in the street and, from the unexpected and secret joy that I experienced at the idea, I discovered how deeply one part of my soul hated them. I planned to burst the tyres of invalid carriages, to go and shout 'filthy poor' under scaffolding where builders were working, and to smack young children in the métro. I dreamed of all this, but didn't do it; or, if I did do something of the sort, I have forgotten it. The fact remains that the very word 'justice' threw me into a strange fury. Of course, I continued to use it in my court speeches. But I had my revenge by publicly declaiming against the humanitarian spirit: I announced the publication of a manifesto that would denounce the oppression that the oppressed inflict on decent people. One day when I was eating lobster on the terrace of a restaurant and a beggar bothered me, I called the owner to get rid of him, and loudly applauded this law enforcer when he said: 'You're being a nuisance. After all, put yourself in the place of these ladies and gentlemen!' I also told whoever wanted to listen that I regretted that it was not possible any longer to act like the Russian landowner whose strength of character I admired: he had his peasants whipped if they saluted him or if they did not – to punish what he considered to be equal cases of effrontery.

However, I recall more serious excesses. I started to compose an 'Ode to the Police' and an 'Apotheosis of the Guillotine'. In particular, I made a point of visiting regularly those specialized cafés where our professional humanists foregather. Needless to say, my clean past record ensured me a warm welcome. There, without seeming to, I would let slip an expletive: 'Thank God!', I would say; or, more simply: 'My God . . .' You know our bistro atheists: shy as kids taking their first communion. The utterance of this frightfulness would be followed by a moment of stupefaction. They would look at one another in amazement; then all hell broke loose: some would rush out of the café, while others clucked away indignantly without listening, and all went into convulsions, like the Devil being sprinkled with holy water.

You must find this childish. Yet there may have been a serious purpose behind these jokes. I wanted to reshuffle the cards and above all, yes, I wanted to destroy that flattering reputation, the idea of which sent me into a fury. 'A man like you . . .', people would say to me, kindly, and I would blanch. I didn't want their good opinion any longer, because it was not general – and how could it be general, since I didn't share it? So it was better to cover everything – judgement and good opinion – with a mantle of ridicule. In any event, I had to free myself from the feeling that was stifling me. I wanted to break up the mannequin that I presented to the world wherever I went, and lay open to scrutiny what was in its belly. I also remember a talk that I was due to give to a group of young trainee lawyers. Irritated by the incredible praise heaped on me by the Bar Association president who introduced me, I could not hold out for long. I started with the enthusiasm and feeling that was expected of me – which I had no trouble delivering to order. Then, suddenly, I began to advise 'transference of guilt' as a tactic for the defence. Not that form of 'transference of guilt', I said, which has been perfected by modern inquisitions where a thief and an honest man are tried at the same time so that the latter can be made responsible for the crimes of the former. What I meant, on the contrary, was defending the thief by bringing out the crimes of the honest man, in the event, the lawyer. I explained very clearly what I meant by this:

'Imagine I had agreed to defend some sweet little chap who had commited murder out of jealousy. "Gentlemen of the jury,"

I should say, "consider what an excusable thing it is to lose one's temper when one sees one's ordinary good nature put to the test by the malignity of the fair sex. Isn't it, on the contrary, a more serious matter to stand on this side of the bar, in lawyer's robes, without ever having been good-hearted or suffered from being duped? I am free, not subject to your penalties, yet who am I? A sun-citizen where pride is concerned, a goat in lust, a pharaoh in anger, a king in idleness. So I haven't killed anyone? Not yet, perhaps! But have I not let many deserving creatures die? Perhaps. And perhaps I am about to do the same again, while this man – look at him – will never repeat his crime. He is still astonished at what he has done."'

My young colleagues found this speech a little disturbing. After a moment, they decided to laugh at it. They were entirely re-assured when I got to my conclusion in which I eloquently spoke about the individual and his presumed rights. That day, habit proved the stronger.

Repeating this mild indiscretion, I only managed to disconcert opinion a little. Not to disarm it, or most of all to disarm myself. The astonishment that I usually met with in my listeners and their rather reticent embarrassment, a bit like the embarrassment that you are showing now – no, don't deny it – brought me no peace of mind. You see, it is not enough to accuse oneself to relieve oneself of guilt; otherwise, I should be as innocent as a lamb. You have to accuse yourself in a certain way, which I took a long time to perfect and which I did not discover until I was in the most abject and neglected state. Up to then, laughter continued to hover around me and my unconcerted efforts could not deprive it of its benevolent, almost affectionate quality, which I found hurtful.

But I think the tide is coming in. Our boat will soon be leaving and day is drawing to a close. Look, the doves are massing up there. They squeeze together, hardly moving, and the light goes down. Shall we stop talking, to savour this rather sinister moment of the day? No, you're interested in what I have to say? You're very honest. Actually, from now on I may really start to interest you. Before I explain about judges-penitent, I have to speak of debauchery and 'little ease'.

You're wrong, dear fellow, the boat is going at a good pace. But the Zuyder Zee is a dead sea, or almost. With its flat shores, lost in the mist, one can't tell where it starts or ends. So we're proceeding with no points of reference and we can't assess our speed. We're going forward, but nothing changes. This is not sailing, but a dream.

I had the opposite impression when I was in the Aegean. New islands were constantly appearing on the rim of the horizon. Their treeless spines marked the limit of the sky while their rocky shores stood out clearly against the sea. No confusion there: in the sharp light, everything was a landmark. And even though our little boat was moving slowly, I had the impression of leaping from one island to the next, without pausing, night and day, along the crest of the short, cool waves in a race full of foam and laughter. Since that time, Greece has been with me constantly, drifting at the edge of my memory, untiringly . . . There, now, I'm drifting myself, I'm waxing lyrical! Stop me, dear fellow, I beg you.

By the way, do you know Greece? No? Just as well. Tell me, what would we do there? It needs a pure heart. Do you know that, there, friends walk along the street, in pairs, holding hands. Yes: the women stay at home and you see respectable, mature men, with moustaches, gravely striding along the pavement, their

61

fingers locked in those of a friend. In the East, too, sometimes? If you say so. But tell me: would you take my hand in the streets of Paris? I'm joking. We have a sense of propriety, the dirt makes us starchy. Before appearing in public in the Greek islands, we would have to take a long wash. The air is virginal, the sea and pleasure transparent. And we . . .

Let's sit down on these deckchairs. What a mist! I stopped, I believe, as we were getting to the 'little ease'. Yes, I'll tell you what it is. After a struggle, after exhausting all my fine, insolent manners, and discouraged by the futility of my efforts, I decided to leave the society of men. No, no, I didn't look for a desert island; there aren't any of them left. I just took refuge among women. You know, they really don't condemn any weakness: they rather try to humilate us or to disarm our strength. This is why woman is the reward, not of the warrior, but of the criminal. She is his port, his harbour: usually he is arrested in a woman's bed. Is she not all that remains to us of the earthly paradise? I was adrift, so I went to my natural haven. But I didn't make any more speeches. I was still acting a little, out of habit, but I lacked inventiveness. I am not sure if I should admit this: I'm afraid of uttering further obscenities. But I really feel that at that time I was experiencing the need for love. Disgusting, no? In any case, I had a vague sense of pain, a sort of deprivation that made me more empty and allowed me, partly through obligation, partly through curiosity, to undertake some commitments. Since I needed to love and be loved, I thought I was in love. In other words, I played the fool.

I often caught myself asking a question which, as a man of experience, I had always avoided up to then; I heard myself asking: 'Do you love me?' You know that, in such cases, it is customary to reply: 'And you?' If I were to say yes, I would find myself committed beyond my real feelings. If I dared to say no,

I risked no longer being loved, and this pained me. The greater the threat to the feeling in which I had hoped to find rest, the greater the demands I made on my partner. I was thus induced to make more and more explicit promises, to the point where I would demand a more and more extensive feeling from my heart. In this way I conceived a false passion for a delightful scatterbrain who had made such a careful study of women's magazines that she spoke of love with the certainty and conviction of an intellectual describing the future classless society. As you well know, such conviction is contagious. I experimented with talking about love myself and ended by persuading myself – at least, until the moment when she became my mistress and I realized that the romantic press, though it teaches you to speak about love, does not teach you how to make it. After loving a parrot, I had to sleep with a snake. So I looked elsewhere for the love promised by books, which I had never encountered in life.

But I was out of training. For more than thirty years, I had been loving only myself. How could one expect to lose such a habit? I didn't; I remained hovering on the brink of passion. I made more and more promises. I engaged in simultaneous love affairs as in earlier times I had enjoyed multiple affairs of lust. This meant that I piled up more unhappiness for others than in the time of my supreme indifference. Did I tell you that, in her despair, my parrot wanted to starve herself to death? Fortunately, I arrived in time and resigned myself to holding her hand until she met the engineer, greying at the temples and fresh from a trip to Bali, whom she had read about in her favourite weekly magazine. In any event, far from being transported and absolved in an eternity of passion, as they say, I merely added to the weight of my sins and my confusion. I conceived such a horror of love that for years I could not hear 'La Vie en rose' or Wagner's *Tristan und Isolde* without it grating on me. So I tried in some way to give up women and to live in a state of chastity. After all, their friendship ought to be enough for me. But that meant giving up the game. Aside from desire, women bored me to a quite unexpected extent and, evidently, I bored them too. No more acting, no more theatre: undoubtedly, I was in the realm of truth; but truth, dear friend, is utterly tedious.

Despairing of love and chastity, I finally decided that what remained was debauchery, which can very well replace love, suppress laughter, restore silence and, above all, confer immortality. You see, at a certain degree of lucid intoxication, lying between two whores, emptied of all desire, hope is no longer a torture: the mind dominates all ages and the pain of living is for ever past. In a sense, I had always lived a life of debauchery, since I had never ceased to desire immortality. Was this not the essence of my character and also the outcome of the great self-love that I spoke of? Yes, I was dying to become immortal. I loved myself too much not to desire that the precious object of my love should never vanish. Since – to one who is fully awake and a little self-aware – there seems to be no good reason why immortality should be conferred on a salacious monkey, it is necessary to obtain substitutes for immortality. Because I desired eternal life, I slept with whores and drank for whole nights on end. The next morning, of course, I had the bitter taste of mortality in my mouth; but for long hours I had glided blissfully. Dare I confess this? I still have sweet memories of some nights when I went to a sordid nightclub to meet one quick-change dancer who dignified me with her favours – and for whose honour I even picked a fight one evening with a boastful pimp. Every night, I would display myself at the counter, in the red light and dust of this house of delight, lying like a fairground quack and drinking long and hard. I would wait for dawn, then collapse at last into the still unmade bed of my princess who gave herself up mechanically to pleasure, then immediately fell asleep. Daylight softly arrived to light the scene of this disaster and I would be found standing, motionless, in a sunrise of glory.

To be honest, alcohol and women have given me the only release I deserved. I am entrusting this secret to you, dear friend; don't be afraid to make use of it; then you will see that true debauchery is liberating because it creates no obligation. In it, one possesses only oneself, so it remains the chosen occupation of those who are great lovers of their own persons. It is a jungle, with no future or past, above all with no promises or immediate sanctions. The places where it happens are cut off from the world: you abandon fear, like hope, as you enter. You don't have to make conversation. What you have come for can be had without words and even, often – it's true – without money. I beg you, allow me to pay tribute in particular to those unknown, forgotten women who helped me at that time. Even now, mixed in with the memories I have of them, there is something close to respect.

In any case, I took full advantage of this liberation. I could even be seen in a hotel dedicated to what is called sin, living at the same time with a prostitute of mature years and a young woman of the highest rank in society. I played the courtly squire with the former and helped the other to learn a little about the realities of life. Unfortunately, the prostitute had a very middle-class character: she has since agreed to write her memoirs for a scandal sheet that is very modern in its outlook. As for the young girl, she got married in order to satisfy her unfettered lusts and find an outlet for her remarkable gifts. I am also more than a little proud of having been accepted as an equal at the time by a guild of men of whom too much ill is often spoken. I shall pass over that: you know that even very intelligent people feel flattered at being able to empty one bottle more than the next man. In the end, I might have found peace and deliverance in this merry dissipation. But here, too, I ran up against an obstacle in myself. It was my liver, on this occasion, and such terrible exhaustion that it has still not left me. You pretend to be immortal and, after a few weeks, you don't even know if you will be able to last as far as the next day.

The only benefit of that experience, when I gave up my nocturnal exploits, was that life became less painful to me. The fatigue that was eating away at my body had at the same time worn down much of my sensitivity. Every excess decreases vitality, and thus suffering. There is nothing frenzied about debauchery, despite what people believe. It is merely a prolonged sleep. You may have noticed that a man who really suffers from jealousy cannot wait to sleep with the woman, despite believing that she has betrayed him. Of course, what he wants is to make sure once again that his precious treasure still belongs to him. He wishes to possess it, as people say. But it's also because immediately afterwards, he feels less jealous. Actually, physical jealousy is an effect of imagination at the same time as a judgement against oneself. We attribute the same bad thoughts to our rival as we ourselves have had in those circumstances. Fortunately, an excess of pleasure debilitates the imagination as well as the judgement, so pain is eased along with virility, and for the same space of time. For the same reason, adolescents lose their metaphysical anxieties with their first mistress, and some marriages, which are officially sanctioned orgies, at the same time become the dull hearses of daring and invention. Yes, my dear fellow, bourgeois marriage has put slippers on the country and will soon take it to the doors of death.

Am I exaggerating? No, but I am straying from the point. I'd just like to tell you the positive outcome for me from that month of debauchery. I was living in a sort of fog in which laughter was dulled until eventually I could no longer perceive it. The indifference that already took up such a large space in me met with no further resistance and its sclerosis spread. No more feelings! An even temper, or rather no temper at all. Tubercular lungs are cured when they dry out and gradually asphyxiate their fortunate owner. So it was with me: I was peacefully dying of my cure. I still lived by my trade, though my reputation was damaged by my intemperate language, and the regular exercise of my profession was compromised by the irregularities of my life. However, it is interesting to observe that I was blamed less for my nocturnal excesses than for my provocative outbursts. The purely verbal references to God that I sometimes made in my pleas in court made my clients suspicious. No doubt they were afraid that heaven would be less qualified to look after their interests than an advocate well-versed in the law; and from there to the conclusion that I would only refer to God when I didn't know what I was talking about, was only a step. My clients took the step and grew fewer. Occasionally, I did still make appearances in court. Sometimes, forgetting that I no longer believed in what I was saying, I would make a good speech. I was carried away by my own voice and, though without soaring as I used to do, I rose a little above the ground – hedge-hopping. Outside work, I saw few people, just about keeping alive one or two exhausted liaisons. I would sometimes even spend evenings of pure friendship, without desire being involved, with the difference that, resigned to boredom, I scarcely listened to what was being said. I put on a little weight and eventually managed to believe that the crisis was over. All that remained was to grow old.

However, one day, during a voyage that I had given as a present to a friend, without telling her that I was doing so to celebrate my cure, I found myself on a cruise ship – on the top deck, of course. Suddenly, far off, I noticed a black spot on the iron-grey ocean. I immediately turned away and my heart started to beat faster. When I forced myself to look, the black spot had vanished. I was going to shout, to call for help – ridiculously – when I saw it again. It was one of those patches of rubbish that ships leave in their wake. Yet I had not been able to bear looking at it: I immediately thought of a drowned person. It was then that, without protest, as one resigns oneself to an idea that one has long known to be true, I realized that the shout I had heard many years earlier echoing across the Seine behind me had not ceased to travel across the world, carried by the river towards the waters of the Channel and over the limitless expanse of the oceans, and that it had been waiting for me until the day when I encountered it. I realized, too, that it would continue to wait for me on the seas and the rivers, in short, wherever there was the bitter water of my baptism. And here, too, tell me: are we not on the sea? On that flat, monotonous, endless sea which merges into the edges of the land? How can you believe that we shall reach Amsterdam? We shall never get out of this vast font. Listen! Can't you hear the cries of invisible gulls? If they are crying to us, then what are they calling us towards?

But they are the same that were crying, calling already on the Atlantic on the day when I finally realized I was not cured, I was still trapped and I had to resign myself to it. The glorious life was over, but so too were the ragings and convulsions. I had to live in 'little ease'. That's right: you don't know about the dungeon known in the Middle Ages as 'little ease'. Usually, they left you there for life. It was different from other prison cells because of its clever dimensions: it was not high enough to stand up in, but not wide enough to lie down. You had to adopt an awkward position and live diagonally. Asleep, you slumped, awake you squatted. My friend, there was genius – and I use the word advisedly – in such a simple invention. Every day, through the unchanging pressure cramping his body, the prisoner learned to know his guilt, and learned that innocence is the joyful stretching of one's limbs. Can you imagine a frequenter of the heights, the upper decks, in such a cell? What? You could live in one of those cells and be innocent? Unlikely, most unlikely! Or else my argument would take a tumble. I am not prepared to harbour for a single second the idea that an innocent person should be reduced to living as a hunchback. In any case, we cannot be certain of anyone's innocence, while we can confidently pronounce everyone guilty. Each man bears witness to the crime of all the others: this is my faith and hope.

Believe me, religions are wrong when they start to moralize and sound off with their commandments. We have no need of God to create guilt or to punish. Our fellow men are enough, with our help. You speak about the Last Judgement. Allow me, with all due respect, to laugh. I am awaiting it resolutely: I have known the worst it can offer, which is the judgement of men. For them, there are no extenuating circumstances and even good intentions are attributed to criminal ones. At least, you must have heard of the spitting cell that one nation thought up recently to prove that it was the greatest on earth? A brick box in which the prisoner is standing upright, but cannot move. The solid door that seals him into his cement shell stops at the level of his chin, so all that can be seen is his face, on which each warder spits copiously. The prisoner, cramped in his cell, cannot wipe himself, even though he is allowed to shut his eyes. Well, that, my good fellow, is an invention of man. They did not need God to dream up that little masterpiece.

What, then? So, the only use of God is to confirm innocence, and to my mind religion is more a great laundering operation, which is what it was, briefly, for barely three years, and at the time it wasn't called religion. Since then, there's been no soap left, our noses are dirty and we've been blowing them for one another. All dunces, all punished, let's spit on one another and off we go to little ease! It's a question of who spits first, that's all. I'll tell you a great secret, dear fellow. Don't wait for the Last Judgement, it takes place every day.

No, it's nothing, I'm shivering a bit in this accursed damp. Anyway, we're there. That's it. After you. But stay a bit longer, do, and come with me. I haven't finished, I must go on. That's what's difficult: going on. Now, do you know why they crucified him, the other fellow, the one you may be thinking of right now? Well, there were any number of reasons for it. There are always reasons for a man's murder. What's impossible, on the contrary, is to justify letting him continue to live. That's why there are always lawyers for the prosecution and only sometimes for the defence. But alongside the reasons that have been very well explained to us over the past two thousand years, there was one great reason for that frightful agony, and I can't see why it is so carefully concealed. The real reason is that he knew, himself, that he was not entirely innocent. While he might not have carried the burden of the sin of which he was accused, he had committed others, even if he did not know what they were. Anyway, did he really not know? He was at the source, after all. He must have heard speak of a certain massacre of the innocents. Why were the children of Judea massacred while his parents were taking him to a safe place, unless it was because of him? Of course, he didn't want it to happen. He was appalled by those bloodstained soldiers and children cut in half. But being who he was, I am sure that he could not forget them. And the sadness that one perceives in everything he does: was that not the incurable melancholy of a man who could hear all night long the voice of Rachel wailing for her children and refusing any consolation? The lamentation rose into the night: Rachel calling to her children, who had been killed for him, while he was alive!

Knowing what he did, understanding everything about mankind – oh, who would have believed that the crime is not so much to make someone die as not to die oneself! – confronted day and night by his innocent crime, it became too hard for him to sustain himself and carry on. It would be better to have done with it, not to defend oneself, to die in order not to be alone in life, to go somewhere else where, perhaps, he would be supported. He was not supported, he complained of it and, to finish it off, he was censured. Yes, it's the third evangelist, I think, who began to suppress his complaint. 'Why have you abandoned me?' was a seditious cry, wasn't it? So, give us the scissors! And note that if Luke had not suppressed it, the matter would have passed more or less unnoticed; in any case, it would not have taken on such importance. That's how the censor advertises what he condemns. The order of the world, too, is ambiguous.

That doesn't alter the fact that the person censored wasn't able to go on. And I know what I'm talking about, dear fellow. There was a time when, at any given moment, I did not know how I should reach the next one. Yes, in this world one can make war, play at love, torture one's fellow man, show off in the newspapers or merely speak ill of one's neighbour while knitting. But in some cases carrying on, just carrying on, is the superhuman achievement. And he was not superhuman, you can believe me on that. He cried out in his agony, and that is why I love him, my friend who died without knowing.

The sad thing is that he left us alone, to carry on whatever happens, even when we are nestling in the little ease, knowing ourselves what he knew, but incapable of doing what he did and dying like him. Of course, we have tried to get a little help from his death. After all, it was a stroke of genius to tell us: 'You're no shining examples, and that's a fact. Very well, let's not quibble about it! We'll get rid of that in one fell swoop, on the cross!' But too many people are now climbing up on the cross just so that they can be seen from further away, even if in doing so they have to trample a little on the one who has already been there for so long. Too many people have decided to do without generosity in practising charity. Oh, the injustice, the injustice that has been done to him: it makes my heart bleed!

Well, well, I'm at it again, I'm going to make a speech. Forgive me, and accept that I have my reasons. A few streets away from here, you know, there's a museum called 'Our Lord in the Attic'. In former times, they used to make their catacombs under the roof. Well, what could they do: the cellars here get flooded. But, have no fear, nowadays their Lord is no longer in the attic or in the cellar. They have hoisted him up on the bench, in the depth of their hearts, and they smite, above all they judge, they judge in his name. He spoke gently to the sinner: 'Neither do I condemn thee.' No matter, they do condemn, they absolve no one. In the Lord's name, here are your dues. Lord? He didn't ask for so much, my friend. He wanted to be loved, nothing more. Of course, there are some people who love him, even among the Christians. But not a lot. Actually, he foresaw that; he had a sense of humour. Peter, you know, the scaredy cat, that Peter, denied him: 'I know not this man of whom ye speak . . . I know not what thou sayest . . .' and so on. Really: that was a bit much. And he made a pun: 'On this rock, I shall build my church.' It would be hard to find a more pointed irony, don't you think? But no, they are still triumphant! 'You see, he said so!' Certainly, he did; he knew the question thoroughly. And then he went away for ever, leaving them to judge and condemn, with a pardon on their lips and a sentence in their hearts.

Because one can't say that there is no longer any pity – great heavens, we never cease talking about it! – just that no one is acquitted any longer. Judges are swarming over the corpse of innocence, judges of every species, those of Christ and Antichrist, who as it happens are the same, all reconciled in little ease. We mustn't blame Christians alone; the rest are also involved. Do you know what has become of a house in this town, one of those that Descartes used to live in? A mental asylum. Yes: general delirium and persecution. And of course, we are obliged to include ourselves. You will have noticed that I spare nothing and I know that you, for your part, agree with me. In that case, as we are all judges, we are guilty before each other, all Christs in our lousy way, crucified one by one, and always without knowing. Or we should be if I, Clamence, had not discovered the way out, the only solution, in short, the truth . . .

No, I'm stopping, dear friend, don't worry! Anyway, I'm leaving you here, we've reached my door. You see, when one is alone, and exhausted to boot, it's easy to think you're a prophet. And that's what I am really, having fled into a wilderness of stone, mists and stagnant waters: an empty prophet for undistinguished times, an Elijah with no messiah, crammed with fever and alcohol, his back stuck against this mouldy door, his finger pointing up at a low sky, calling down curses on the heads of lawless men who cannot bear to be judged. Because they can't bear it, my dear fellow, and that's the whole of the matter. A person who obeys a law is not afraid of judgement: it restores him to a system in which he believes. But the greatest of human torments is to be judged without a law. Yet this is the torment in which we find ourselves. Deprived of their natural restraint, judges, let loose haphazardly, are working double time. So we have to try to go faster than they do, don't we? The result is a mighty pandemonium. More and more prophets and healers appear, rushing to produce a good law or a faultless organization, before the earth is a desert. Fortunately, I am here now! I am the end and the beginning, I announce the law. In short, I am a judge-penitent.

Yes, yes, I'll tell you tomorrow what that fine profession consists of. You're leaving the day after, so we haven't got much time. Come to my house, would you? Ring three times. You're going back to Paris? It's a long way, Paris, and beautiful; I haven't forgotten it. I remember dusk there, at about this time of year: darkness falls, dry and rustling, over the rooftops blue with smoke; the city gives off a dull rumbling sound and the river seems to have turned back in its course. I used to wander through the streets, then. They, too, are wandering, now, I know! They are wandering, pretending to be in a hurry to get back to their weary housewives and their stern homes . . . Oh, my friend: do you know what he is, that solitary creature, wandering in the great cities . . . ?

I'm embarrassed to receive you lying down. It's nothing: a slight temperature that I'm treating with gin. I'm used to this particular fever: malaria, I think, which I picked up when I was pope. No, I'm only half joking. I know what you think: it's hard to distinguish what's true from what's false in the things I say. I have to confess you're right. Even I myself . . . Look, someone I used to know would divide people into three categories: those who prefer to have nothing to hide rather than being obliged to lie; those who prefer to lie rather than have nothing to hide; and finally those who like lying and concealing at the same time. I'll let you choose which category fits me best.

What does it matter, after all? Don't lies in the end put us on the path to truth? And don't my stories, true or false, point to the same conclusion? Don't they have the same meaning? So, what does it matter whether they are true or false if, in either case, they signify what I have been and what I am? One can sometimes see more clearly in a person who is lying than in one who is telling the truth. Like light, truth dazzles. Untruth, on the other hand, is a beautiful dusk that enhances everything. Finally, take this how you like, I was called 'pope' in a prison camp.

Please sit down. You're looking at the room. It's bare, I know, but clean. A Vermeer, with no furniture or saucepans. Without books, too: I gave up reading long ago. At one time my house was full of half-read books. That's as disgusting as people who take one piece of *foie gras* and throw the rest away. In any case, I only like confessions nowadays, and the authors of confessions write chiefly in order not to confess, saying nothing of what they know. When they pretend to be owning up, that's the moment to beware: they're putting make-up on the corpse. Believe me, I'm a craftsman. So I stopped: no more books, no more useless objects, either, just the bare necessities, neat and polished like a coffin. In any case, with these Dutch beds that are so hard, and their immaculate sheets, it's like dying in a shroud already, embalmed in purity.

So you want to know about my papal adventures? Quite ordinary, you know. Shall I be strong enough to talk about them to you? Yes, I feel my temperature is going down. It was all so long ago. It happened in Africa where war was raging thanks to Mr Rommel. No, I wasn't involved, don't worry. I'd already got out of the one in Europe. Called up, of course, but I never saw a shot fired. In a way, I'm sorry. Perhaps it would have changed a lot of things. The French Army didn't need me at the front. They just asked me to take part in the retreat. Afterwards, I caught up with Paris again and the Germans. I was tempted by the Resistance: people were just starting to talk about it at the time when I discovered I was a patriot. That makes you smile? You're wrong. I made the discovery in a corridor in the métro, at Châtelet. A dog had got lost in the maze there, a large dog with bristles, a torn ear and laughing eyes, he was darting around, sniffing the ankles of passers-by. I have a long and very well-established affection for dogs. I like them because they always forgive. I called this one and he stopped, clearly won over, wagging his tail with enthusiasm a few yards away from me. At that moment, a young German soldier came along briskly and overtook me. Reaching the dog, he patted its head. Without hesitating, the creature followed after him with the same degree of enthusiasm, and they disappeared together. From the irritation and the kind of fury that I felt against the German soldier, I had to acknowledge that my reaction was patriotic. If the dog had followed a French civilian, I shouldn't even have thought about it, whereas now I imagined the friendly creature becoming the mascot of a German regiment, and that made me furious. It was clear proof. I went to the Southern Zone, intending to find out about the Resistance. But when I got there and did find out, I thought again. The whole business seemed a bit crazy to me and, if you want to know, romantic. Most of all, I don't think that underground work suited either my personality or my liking for airy heights. It seemed to me that I was being asked to make a tapestry in a cellar, working days and nights on end, while waiting for some brutes to discover me, unpick my tapestry and then drag me into another cellar to beat me to death. I admired those who engaged in this heroism in the depths, but I couldn't do the same myself.

So I went to North Africa, with some vague idea of getting to London. But in Africa the situation was confused and both of the warring factions seemed to me equally right, so I abstained. I can see from your look that you think I'm glossing rather quickly over these significant details. Well, let's say that having appreciated you at your true worth, I am glossing quickly over them so that you will find it all the easier to take them in. Anyway, I eventually reached Tunisia, where a dear friend found work for me. This was a very intelligent woman who was involved in cinema. I followed her to Tunis and only learned the real nature of her employment in the days following the Allied disembarkment in Algeria. That day, she was arrested by the Germans; so was I, but without intending it. I don't know what became of her. In my case, they did not harm me, and I realized, after some very worrying moments, that it was just a security measure. I was interned near Tripoli in a camp where thirst and deprivation caused more suffering than ill-treatment. I won't describe it to you. We children of the half century don't need a diagram to imagine that kind of place. A hundred and fifty years ago, people would get sentimental about lakes and forests. Today, we have the lyricism of the prison cell. So, I'll leave you to fill in the details. You only need a few: heat, sun directly overhead, flies, sand, no water.

With me was a young Frenchman, who was a religious believer. Yes, it's definitely a fairytale: something along the lines of du Guesclin, if you like. He had gone from France to Spain to fight. The Catholic general interned him and, having seen that in Franco's camps the chickpeas were, if I dare say it, blessed by Rome, plunged him into deep melancholy. Neither the sky of Africa, where he ended up later, nor the idleness of the camp brought him out of this sadness. But his thoughts, and the sun, too, somewhat unhinged him. One day when, in a tent running with molten lead, the dozen or so of us were panting among the flies, he launched into another diatribe against the Roman, as he called him. He looked at us with a distracted air, wearing several days' growth of beard. His naked torso was dripping with sweat and his hands were constantly playing on the visible keyboard of his ribs. He announced that we needed a new pope who lived among the poor and needy, instead of praying on his throne, and the sooner the better. He stared at us with his wild eyes, shaking his head. 'Yes,' he repeated, 'as soon as possible!' Then he suddenly calmed down and, in a dull voice, said that we had to choose this pope from among ourselves, to take a rounded man with his vices and his virtues, and swear obedience to him, on the sole condition that he would agree to keep the community of our sufferings alive in himself and in the others.

'Who among us has the most weakness?' he asked. As a joke,

I raised my hand and I was the only one to do so. 'Very well, Jean-Baptiste will do.' No, he didn't say that, because in those days I had a different name. He announced that at least to put oneself forward as I had done implied the greatest virtue and he proposed electing me. The others agreed, playing the game, but also with a hint of seriousness. The truth is that du Guesclin had impressed us. It seems to me that I myself was not entirely joking. First of all, I felt that my litle prophet was right; and then with the sun, the exhausting work and the struggle for water, well, we weren't any of us quite normal. The outcome was that I exercised my pontificate for several weeks, more and more seriously.

What did it consist of? Why, I was something like a group leader or the secretary of a party cell. In any case, the others, even those who were non-believers, became accustomed to obeying me. Du Guesclin was in pain; I administered his suffering. I did notice that being pope was not as easy as you might think, and that's something I remembered yesterday, after saying so many scornful things about our brothers, the judges. The main problem in the camp was distributing water. Other groups had formed, along political and professional lines, and everyone gave preference to his comrades. So I was led to prefer mine, which was already a small concession. Even among us I could not maintain perfect equality. I favoured one or another, according to their state of health or the work they had to do. These distinctions went a long way, believe me. But now, to be honest, I'm tired and I'd rather not think about that time. Let's just say that I brought it all back to square one on the day when I drank the water of one of our dying comrades. No, no, it wasn't du Guesclin; I think he was already dead, he sacrificed himself too much. And then, if he had been there, I should have held out longer, through love of him, because I loved him, yes, I loved him ... at least, that's how it seems to me. The thing that's certain is that I drank the water, convincing myself that the others needed me more than the man – who was going to die in any case – so I ought to conserve myself for them. There, dear friend, that's how empires and churches are born, under the sun of death. And to put you straight on something I said yesterday, I'm going to tell you the great idea that came to me while I was speaking of all this – and I don't know myself any longer if I experienced it or dreamed it. My great idea is that the pope must be forgiven. First of all, he needs it more than anyone else. And then it's the only way to set oneself above him ...

Now, have you locked the door properly? Yes? Would you be good enough to check? Forgive me, I've got a key complex. When I'm going to sleep, I can never remember if I've shot the bolt. Every evening, I have to get up and make sure. As I told you, you can't be certain of anything. Don't imagine that this key anxiety is the reaction of a nervous homeowner. In the old days, I used not to lock my flat door or my car. I didn't hide away my money: I wasn't attached to possessions. To tell the truth, I was a little ashamed of having them. I even used to exclaim, with conviction, when I was talking to people: 'Property, gentlemen, is murder!' Not being big-hearted enough to share my wealth with one of the deserving poor, I would leave it available for a potential thief, hoping in that way to correct injustice by chance. Nowadays, I have nothing, so I'm not worried about security, but about myself and my presence of mind. I'd also like to block the door of the tight little universe in which I am king, pope and judge.

Actually, would you like to open that cupboard, please? The painting: yes, take a look at it. Don't you recognize it? *The Just Judges*. Not surprised? Is this a gap in your general knowledge? Though if you read the papers, you'd remember the theft in 1934, from the St Bavon Cathedral in Gand, of one panel from the famous Van Eyck altarpiece, *The Mystic Lamb*. The panel in question was called *The Just Judges*. It showed some judges on horseback on the way to adore the sacred animal. It has been replaced by an excellent copy, because the original was never found. Well, here it is. No, I didn't have anything to do with it. A regular at Mexico City, whom you saw briefly the other night, sold it for a bottle to the gorilla, one drunken evening. Originally, I advised our friend to hang it in a prominent place, and for a long time, while it was being hunted all around the world, the devout judges presided over Mexico City, above the heads of drunks and pimps. Then the gorilla, at my request, stored it here. He was slightly reluctant to do so, but took fright when I explained about it. Since then, the admirable magistrates have been my only companions. You saw what a gap they left, back there, over the bar.

Why didn't I return the panel? There, you see: you think like a cop! Well, I'll answer you as I would an investigating magistrate, if anyone were to find out, at last, that this picture has washed up in my room. Firstly, because it's not mine: it belongs to the landlord at Mexico City who deserves it quite as much as the bishop of Gand. Secondly, because out of all those who file past *The Mystic Lamb*, not one could tell the copy from the original and, consequently, no one has been harmed by what I've done. Thirdly, because in this way I come out on top: false judges are offered to the admiration of the world and I am the only one who knows the true ones. Fourthly, because in this way I too have a chance of being sent to jail, which in some ways is an attractive notion. Fifthly, because these judges are going to meet the Lamb, and there is no longer a Lamb or any innocence, and consequently the clever rogue who stole the panel was an instrument of that unknown justice which we would do well not to thwart. Finally, because in this way, order is restored. With justice definitively separated from innocence, the latter on the cross, the former in the cupboard, I have a free hand to work according to my convictions. I can in all good conscience exercise the difficult profession of judge-penitent on which I have settled after so many disappointments and contradictions. And, since you're leaving, it's time now for me to tell you at last what it is.

First of all, let me sit up so that I can breathe more easily. Oh, I'm so tired! Would you lock my judges up again? Thank you. The profession of judge-penitent is the one that I am exercising at the moment. Usually, my office is at Mexico City, but a great vocation extends beyond the place of work. Even in bed, even when I am running a temperature, I'm working. In reality, this is not a profession that you exercise; you breathe it, constantly. Don't imagine that I've been making these long speeches to you for the past five days just for pleasure. No, I produced enough empty chatter in the old days. Now what I say is guided – guided by the idea, naturally, of making laughter cease, of avoiding personal judgement, although there is apparently no way out. Surely the great thing that stops us escaping from it is that we are the first to condemn ourselves. So we must start by extending condemnation to everyone, without discrimination, so as to start extenuating it.

No excuses, ever, for anyone: that's my principle from the beginning. I deny good intentions, decent mistakes, wrong steps and extenuating circumstances. With me, there is no benediction, no absolutions are handed out. We just do the sums, then: 'It amounts to so much. You're a pervert, a sex maniac, a congenital liar, a pederast, an artist, and so on.' Like that. No frills. So, in philosophy as in politics, I'm in favour of any favour that denies innocence to Man and every practice that treats him as guilty. Dear fellow, in me you see an enlightened supporter of slavery.

Honestly, without it, there can be no definitive solution. I soon realized that. Before, the word freedom was constantly on my lips. I would spread it at breakfast on my bread, chew it all day and exude a breath that was delightfully freedom-fresh. I thumped this key word down on anyone who contradicted me: I had enrolled it in the service of my desires and my power. I murmured it in bed, in the sleeping ears of my women, and it helped me to get them there. I slipped it . . . Wait, I'm getting excited and exaggerating. After all, I have been know to make a more disinterested use of freedom and even – imagine how naive I was – to defend it two or three times, of course without going so far as to die for it, but taking some risks. You must forgive me this rash behaviour: I knew not what I did. I didn't know that freedom is not a reward or a decoration that you toast in champagne. Nor is it a gift, a box of delicacies which will make your mouth water. Oh, no! On the contrary, it's hard graft and a long-distance run, all alone, very exhausting. No champagne, no friends raising their glasses and looking affectionately at you. Alone in a dreary room, alone in the dock before the judges, and alone to make up your mind, before yourself and before the judgement of others. At the end of every freedom there is a sentence, which is why freedom is too heavy to bear, especially when you have a temperature, or you are grieving, or you love nobody.

Ah, my dear fellow, for anyone who is alone, recognizing neither god nor master, the weight of days is awful. So one must choose a master, God being out of fashion now. Besides, the word no longer has any meaning; it's not worth the risk of shocking anyone. Why, our moralists, those who are so serious and love their neighbours: when it comes down to it, nothing distinguishes them from being Christian, except that they don't preach in churches. In your view, what prevents them from converting? Respect, perhaps: the respect of their fellow men, yes, human respect. They don't want to cause a scandal so they keep their feelings to themselves. One atheist I knew, a novelist, used to pray every evening. It didn't make any difference: what a hard time he gave God in his books! What a thrashing, as someone whose name I've forgotten would say! One militant freethinker to whom I confided this information threw his hands heavenwards – actually, without meaning any harm by it: 'It's no news to me,' this apostle sighed. 'They're all like that.' If we're to believe him, eighty per cent of our writers, if only they could do so anonymously, would write and hail the name of God. But they sign their names, according to him, because they love themselves, and they hail nothing, because they hate themselves. As they cannot prevent themselves from judging, they make up for it in morality. In short, they get virtuous satanism. Honestly, this is a peculiar age! Can one really be surprised if people's minds are troubled and that one of my friends, an atheist when he was a perfect husband, was converted when he became an adulterer!

Oh, the sly little devils, actors and hypocrites – and so touching with it! Believe me, they're all like that, even when they set the heavens on fire. Whether they're atheists or staunch believers, Muscovites or Bostonians, they're all Christians, from father to son. But that's just it: there is no father any more, no rules! They're free, so they have to get by as best they can; and since, most of all, they don't want any freedom, or sentences, they pray to have their knuckles rapped, they invent dreadful rules and they rush to build pyres to replace churches. Savonarolas, I tell you. But they only believe in sin, not in grace. They think about it, of course. Grace is what they want – a 'yes', surrender, joy in living and, who knows, because they're sentimental, too, betrothal, a fresh young virgin, an upright man, music . . . Take me, for example – and I'm not sentimental; do you know what I dreamed of? A complete love, of the whole body and heart, day and night, in one continuous embrace, sexual pleasure and emotional exultation, for five years on end, and after that, death. Alas!

So, don't you think, without betrothals or endless love, it will be marriage, brutal, with power and the whip. The main point is that everything should become simple, as it is for a child; that every action should be commanded, and that good and evil should be distinguished in an arbitrary, and therefore clear, manner. And I agree, Sicilian and Javanese though I am, and not the slightest bit Christian, though I do have some friendly feelings towards the very first of them. But on the bridges of Paris, I too learned that I was afraid of freedom. So: long live the master, whoever he may be, to replace the law of heaven. 'Our Father, who are provisionally here . . . Our guides, our deliciously strict masters, oh, you, cruel and beloved leaders . . .' In short, you see, the main idea is not to be free any longer, but to repent and obey a greater knave than you are. When we are all guilty, that will be democracy. Not to mention the fact that we must be revenged for having to die alone. Death is solitary while servitude is collective. The rest get their dues, too, and at the same times as us, which is the important thing. In short, all united, but on our knees, heads bowed.

Isn't it also good to be like the rest of society, and for that doesn't the rest of society have to be like me? Threats, dishonour and the police are the sacraments of that similarity. Then, despised, hunted and constrained, I can reveal my full worth, enjoy being what I am and, in short, be natural. This is why, my dear, after solemnly paying my respects to freedom, I privately decided that it had to be relinquished, to anyone, as quickly as possible. And whenever I can, I preach in my church of Mexico City, inviting the good people to submit and humbly seek out the comforts of slavery, while I present it as the true freedom.

But I'm not mad, I realize that slavery will not be achieved tomorrow. It will be one of the benefits of the future, that's all. Until then, I have to resign myself to the present and look for a solution, if only provisional. So I had to find another means of extending judgement to everyone to lighten the burden on my own shoulders. And I did find it. Would you be good enough to open the window: it's terribly hot in here. But not too much, because I also feel cold. My idea is both simple and productive. How do you put everyone in the pool, so that you can have the right to dry yourself in the sun? Was I to get up in the pulpit, like many of my illustrious contemporaries, and curse the human race? Very dangerous! One day – or one night – laughter breaks out, with no warning. The judgement that you are passing on others eventually blows right back in your face and may do some damage. So what then, you ask? Well, this is the stroke of genius. I found that while we are waiting for our masters and their canes, we ought, like Copernicus, to invert the argument if we are to triumph. Since one could not condemn others without at the same time judging oneself, one should heap accusations on one's own head, in order to have the right to judge others. Since every judge eventually becomes a penitent, one had to take the opposite route and be a professional penitent in order to become a judge. Do you follow? Good. But to make it even clearer, I'll tell you how I work.

First of all, I closed my lawyer's practice, left Paris and travelled. I tried to set up under another name in a place where there would be no shortage of clients. There are lots in the world, but chance, convenience, irony and also the need for a kind of self-mortification, made me choose this capital of waters and fogs, hemmed in with canals, particularly overcrowded and visited by people from all over the world. I set up my practice in a bar in the sailors' quarter. You get a varied clientele in ports. The poor don't visit the richer parts of town, while people of quality always eventually wash up, at least once, as you have seen, in places of ill repute. I keep a special eye open for the middle class, for the bourgeois who has strayed. It's with him that I give my best performance: I'm a virtuoso and he's the one who produces the most refined sound.

So for some time I have been practising my useful profession at Mexico City. As you were able to observe, this consists first of all in making a public confession as often as I can. I accuse myself this way and that. It's not hard, I've got a good memory now. But don't get it wrong: I don't accuse myself crudely, wildly beating my breast. No, I go subtly, with lots of nuance and digressions, adapting what I say to my listener and in the end getting him to take it even further. I mix up things about myself and about others. I take the features we have in common, the experiences that we have undergone together, our shared weaknesses, good manners and, in short, the man of the day as he reigns in myself and others. Out of that, I build up a portrait of everyone and no one. In short, a mask, like a carnival mask, both accurate and stylized, the kind that makes you exclaim: 'Look, I've met *him*!' When the portrait is finished, as it is this evening, then I exhibit it, quite desolate: 'Alas, this is what I am!' The case for the prosecution is over, while at the same time the portrait that I offer my contemporaries becomes a mirror.

In sackcloth and ashes, slowly tearing out my hair, my face ploughed with scratches, but sharp-eyed, I stand before the whole of humankind, going over my shameful actions, ever-conscious of the effect I am having and saying: 'I was the lowest of the low.' Then, imperceptibly, my speech slips from 'I' to 'we'. When I get to the point of saying: 'This is what we are', the switch has been made and I can tell them some home truths. Of course, I'm like them: we're all in the same boat. But I have one superiority over them, which is that I know, and that gives me the right to speak. You can see the advantage, I'm sure. The more I accuse myself, the more I have the right to judge you. Better still: I incite you to judge yourself, which relieves me by that much more. My dear fellow, we are strange and miserable creatures and we have only to go back over our lives to find any number of opportunities to astonish and shock ourselves. Try it. You may be sure that I will listen to your own confession, with a great feeling of fraternity.

Don't laugh! Yes, I could see from the start that you were a difficult customer. But you'll get there in the end, you can't help it. Most of the rest are more emotional than intellectual: they can be disconcerted from the first. With intelligent people, you have to spend more time. You have to explain your system to them in depth. They don't forget about it, they mull it over. One day or another, partly in play, partly through confusion, they spill the beans. Now, you, you're not only intelligent, you look like someone who's been around. But just admit that you feel less happy with yourself today than you did five days ago. Now I'll wait for you to write or come back to see me. Because I'm sure you will come back. You'll find me just the same – why should I change, since I've found the kind of happiness that suits me? I have accepted duplicity, instead of bewailing it. On the contrary, I've settled in it and that's where I've found the comfort that I'd been searching for all my life. After all, when it comes down to it, I was wrong to tell you that the main thing was to avoid judgement. The main thing is to be able to let oneself do anything, while from time to time loudly declaring one's own unworthiness. I allow myself everything, once again, and this time without laughing. I haven't changed my way of life: I still love myself and I still use other people. It's just that confessing my sins permits me to start again with a lighter heart and to gratify myself twice, firstly enjoying my nature, and then a delicious repentance.

Since finding my solution, I abandon myself to everything: women, pride, boredom, resentment and even the fever which I am delighted to feel rising in me at the moment. I am reigning, at last, but for ever. I have again found a summit that I have climbed alone and from where I can judge everyone. Sometimes, now and then, when the night is truly beautiful, I hear a distant laugh and once more experience doubt. But I quickly crush everything – creatures and creation – under the weight of my own infirmity, and I'm my old self again.

So, I'll wait as long as I need to for you to come and pay your respects at Mexico City. Could you take off the blanket? I can't breathe. You will come, won't you? I'll even show you the details of my technique, because I have a kind of affection for you. You'll see how I teach them all night long that they are vile. Actually, I'll start again this evening. I cannot do without it, or deprive myself of those moments when one of them collapses, helped by alcohol, and starts to beat his breast. Then I grow, my dearest fellow, I am on the mountain top with the plain stretching out before my eyes. What intoxication to feel that one is God the Father, handing out definitive testimonials of bad character and behaviour. I am enthroned among my bad angels at the peak of the Dutch heavens and watch the multitude of the Last Judgement rise towards me out of the mists and the damp. Slowly, they drift upwards. I can already see the first of them coming. On his distraught features, half hidden by one hand, I read the sadness of our common condition and the despair of being unable to escape it. As for me, I pity without absolving, I understand without forgiving and above all (ah!) at last I feel adored!

Yes, I'm getting excited. How do you expect me to stay sensibly in bed? I have to be higher up than you; my thoughts uplift me.

These nights, or rather these mornings, because the fall occurs at dawn, I go out and walk briskly along the canals. In the livid sky, the layers of feathers thin out and the doves fly a little higher, while pink light on the crest of the roofs announces the arrival of a new day of my creation. The first tram on the Damrak sounds its bell in the damp air and marks the awakening of life at this extreme end of Europe where, at the same moment, millions of men, my subjects, are painfully rising from their beds, a bitter taste in their mouths, to set off for their joyless labours. Then, gliding in thought above this whole continent which, without knowing it, is subject to me, drinking the absinthe day as it breaks and intoxicated with bad words, I am happy – happy, I tell you – I forbid you not to believe that I am happy, I am happy to die! Oh! Sun, beaches, and the trade winds blowing across the islands: youth, the memory of which brings despair!

Excuse me, I'm going back to bed. I'm afraid I got over-excited, though I'm not crying. Sometimes you lose your way and doubt the evidence, even when you've discovered the secrets of a good life. Of course, my solution is not ideal. But when you don't like your life and know that it has to be changed, you have no choice, do you? How do you manage to be someone else? Impossible. You would have to be no one any longer and forget yourself for someone else, at least once. And how can you do that? Don't be too hard on me. I'm like the old beggar who didn't want to let go of my hand one day on the terrace of a café: 'Oh, Monsieur,' he said. 'It's not that I'm a bad man, but one loses the light.' Yes, we've lost the light, the mornings, the holy innocence of the man who forgives himself.

Look at the snow falling. I must go out! Amsterdam sleeping in the white night, the canals of dark jade under their little snowy bridges, the empty streets and my muffled steps: it would be purity, a fleeting moment, before tomorrow's mud. Look at the huge flakes fluffed up against the window panes. It's the doves, surely. At last, those dear doves, they've made up their minds to come down and cover the water and the roofs with a thick layer of feathers; they're fluttering against all the windows. What an invasion! Let's hope they're bringing good news. Everyone will be saved, no? Not only the elect. Wealth and sorrow will be shared and, for example, you will sleep on the ground every night from now on, for my sake. The full works, huh? Come on, admit that you'd be struck dumb if a chariot came down from heaven to carry me off or if the snow suddenly caught fire. You don't believe in it? Nor do I. But I still have to go out.

All right, all right, I'll stay here quietly, don't worry! And don't put too much trust in my emotional outpourings, or my wild outbursts: they're contrived. Ah, now that you're going to tell me about yourself, I want to know if I've achieved one of the aims of my gripping confession. I keep hoping that the person I'm talking to will be a policeman and that he'll arrest me for the theft of *The Just Judges*. No one can arrest me for the other things, can they? But that theft does come within the purview of the law and I've done everything I could to make myself an accomplice: I'm the receiver of the painting and I show it to anyone who wants to see it. So if you were to arrest me, that would be a good start. Then perhaps they'd take care of the rest; for instance, they might guillotine me, I wouldn't be afraid of dying any longer, I'd be saved. And you could lift my newly severed head above the crowd, so that they could recognize themselves in it and I would dominate them once more, as an example to them. All would be consummated: unseen, unknown, I should have finished my career as a false prophet crying in the desert and refusing to come forth.

But of course you're not a policeman: that would be too easy. What? Ah, I thought as much! So that strange affection I felt for you did make sense. You are a member of a fine profession, a lawyer in Paris. I knew we belonged to the same breed. Aren't we all the same, continually talking, addressing no one, constantly raising the same questions, even though we know the answers before we start? So, tell me, please, what happened to you one evening on the banks of the Seine and how you managed never to risk your life. Say the words that for years have not ceased to echo through my nights and that I shall finally speak through your mouth: 'Young woman! Throw yourself in the water again so that I might have once more the opportunity to save us both!' A second time – huh! That would be rash! Just imagine, dear colleague, if someone were to take us at our word. You'd have to do it. Brrr . . . The water's so cold! But don't worry. It's too late now, it will always be too late. Thank goodness!